LAWFULLY ADORED

JENNA BRANDT

COPYRIGHT

Cover design by Josephine Blake with photo copyright by Period Images and 123rf.com

INTRODUCTION TO THE LAWKEEPERS SERIES

There's just something fascinating about a man wearing an emblem of authority. The way the light gleams off that shiny star on his badge makes us stare with respect. Couple that with a uniform hugging his body in just the right way, confidence, and mission to save and protect, it's no wonder we want to know what lies underneath.

Yes, what echoes deep inside those beating hearts is inspiring. Certainly appealing. Definitely enticing. Although those ripped muscles and strong shoulders can make a woman's heart skip a beat—or two—it takes a strong, confident person to choose to love someone who risks it all every day. Anyone willing to become part of a lawkeeper's world might have a story of their own to tell.

The undeniable charisma lawmen possess make all of us pause and take note. It's probably why there are so many movies and TV shows themed around the justice system. We're enthralled by their ability to save babies, help strangers, and rescue damsels in distress. We're captivated by their ability to protect and save, defend the innocent, risk their lives, and face danger without hesitation. Of course, we expect our heroes to stay solid when we're in a mess. We count on them for safety, security, and peace of mind. From yesterday to today, that truth remains constant.

Their valor inspires us, their integrity comforts, and their courage melts our hearts—irresistibly. But there's far more to them than their courageous efforts. How do they deal with the difficulties they face? Can they balance work and life? And how do they find time for love outside their life of service?

We want to invite you on a journey—come with us as we explore the complex lives of the men and women who serve and protect us every day. Join us in a fast-paced world of adventure. Walk into our tight-knit world of close friendships, extended family, and danger—as our super heroes navigate the most treacherous path of all—the road to love.

The Lawkeepers. Historical and modern-day super heroes; men and women of bravery and valor, taking love and law seriously. A multi-author series, sure to lock up your attention and take your heart into custody.

Visit The Lawkeepers on Facebook

Join our mailing list

The Lawkeepers is a multi-author series alternating between historical westerns and contemporary westerns featuring law enforcement heroes that span multiple agencies and generations. Join best-selling authors Jenna Brandt, Lorana Hoopes, Elle E. Kay, Patricia PacJac Caroll, Evangeline Kelly, Ginny Sterling and Barb Goss as they weave captivating, sweet, and inspirational stories of romance and suspense between the lawkeepers — and the women who love them.

The Lawkeepers is a world like no other; a world where lawkeepers and heroes are honored with unforgettable stories, characters, and love.

** Note: Each book in **The Lawkeepers** series is a standalone book, and part of a mini-series of sorts, and you can read them in any order.

Dedicated to

my husband, Dustin, Badge #5654,

who inspired me to create this series.

You're not only my heart and soul,

but my own personal lawkeeper.

ONE

Police officer Aiden O'Connell looked out over the mountain peak at the setting sun and knew only a small window of time remained to find the missing hiker.

Aiden bent down next to his German Shepherd partner, Cooper, allowing him to inspect an area below a cluster of towering pine trees between a set of giant boulders. True to his training, Cooper barked and urged Aiden to follow him up an overgrown hiking trail.

Clear Mountain, Colorado was a popular destination for tourists. The craggy rock formations overlooking the quaint town were a constant attraction for outdoor enthusiasts. Unfortunately, inexperienced hikers would often underestimate the dangers of the area, causing themselves to get hurt or lost.

Aiden and Cooper were one of the only two K-9 search and rescue teams for the entire area. The Clear Mountain Search and Rescue unit was comprised of only three other officers and a sergeant. The constant call-outs to the surrounding mountain areas kept the team busy.

This evening, a call from Boulder came in from a distraught wife. She reported her husband had not returned from his weekend hiking trip. Her concern resulted in deployment of the rescue team.

"K-9 2, this is K-9 1, we aren't having any luck over on this side. What's your status?" a deep male voice echoed out over the radio.

Aiden pulled the receiver for his radio free from his dark blue uniform and pushed the button on the side to talk back. "K-9 1, we might have gotten a possible beat over here." Pulling a map out of his back pocket, Aiden glanced down to confirm his location. He was still getting used to the area after transferring from Boulder County Police a year prior. "We're two clicks from Meadow Ridge near the cluster of pines by the twin boulders."

"Copy that, K-9 2, we're headed over your way."

Like a well-oiled machine, Cooper and Aiden continued to move up the trail with Cooper stopping every few hundred yards to inspect a new area. The west side of the mountain sheared off, leaving only forest on the east side.

Several minutes later, a second German Shepherd came charging in from the right side of Aiden and Cooper. The smaller dog joined Cooper and playfully nipped at him while the same male voice from earlier said, "I think Harley is jealous of Cooper for picking up the scent on this one."

Aiden turned his head to the right, recognizing fellow officer, Zach Turner. "Eh, it's only because Cooper has a couple of years on Harley. Brad did a great job of training her." Aiden noticed that Zach stiffened at the mention of his former partner, so Aiden quickly added, "Harley will catch up soon enough, especially with you handling her, Zach."

"Yeah, but I was hoping to find this hiker on my own, so I could finally secure a date with that female reporter from the Clear Mountain Gazette who keeps following you around."

Aiden shrugged. "You and me both. It would be great if you could get her off my back."

"Man, what is it with you? Have you seen her? She's hot; a solid nine. What? Are you holding out for a ten?"

"No, she just seems more attracted to the badge

than to me and you know I'm not into that," Aiden explained.

"I've never known you to be attracted to anyone since you've been here. When are you going to get over Veronica dumping you?"

Why did Zach have to bring up Veronica? Aiden was regretting his decision in telling his friend about his ex-fiancée. It was a sore subject since she had broken off their engagement for a police captain back in Boulder necessitating his need to transfer to the Clear Mountain police substation.

"Why are you doing this, Veronica?"

"You know why, Aiden," she had said as she packed up the last of the items she kept at his place. "You're gone all the time because of your K-9 position. I'm lonely and want to be with someone who's home every night."

"Give me a couple of years and I will be," he pleaded.

Shaking her brown locks, she stated, "You won't ever leave that job. You love it too much and we both know it."

Aiden crossed his arms, knowing there was more to the story than she was admitting. "And the prestige and money has nothing to do with it?"

Her eyes narrowed into slits as she spat out, "What do you mean by that?"

"I know you dated several patrol officers before one turned into a relationship. Then you met me, and you left Morrison because I made more as a K-9 officer, plus I was

in the news occasionally. You were working your way up the ranks and now you've landed yourself a captain."

"You don't know what you're talking about." The moment she bit her bottom lip, he knew she was lying. It was her tell.

"Keep telling yourself that Veronica, but I know the truth."

Aiden had tried to make it work in Boulder but the constant questions about what happened and the reminder when he saw her new boyfriend made it impossible for him to stay. As soon as a K-9 spot was posted elsewhere, he put in for a transfer.

"I'm over badge bunnies; they're always looking to land a better cop. I'm tired of dating the same type of women who are only interested in the uniform."

"Sure, it's just the uniform. It has nothing to do with your model good looks and list of newsworthy awards," Zach stated with sarcasm and a hint of jealousy. "Man, what I wouldn't give to have your problems. I have to work twice as hard for half as much attention."

Women regularly told Aiden he was attractive, citing his smoldering brown eyes as his best asset. For work, he kept his brown hair trimmed short and his body in good shape.

Aiden looked over at his friend and partner. Zach's rejections didn't stem from a lack of good looks—he was decent looking with black hair and blue eyes—or charm, as he could be charismatic. His problem was that he "worked" too hard, causing most women to shy away. On more than one occasion—to no avail—Aiden had tried to explain to Zach that most women didn't like the hard sell but much preferred a softer approach; not that Aiden cared to make any approach after Veronica burned him.

"You think we're gonna find this guy before we have to turn back?"

"Not sure. Depends how foolish he was," Aiden stated.

"Well, at least this guy told his wife which trail he planned to follow."

"Let's just hope he stuck fairly close to it, but if he had simply stopped by the ranger station, he would have been informed that this trail had been closed to the public."

Several mudslides had washed out sections of the trail, making certain spots impassible. With the closure, the trail wasn't being maintained by the forest rangers. Not only was it unsafe; it was covered with brush and plants, making it difficult to navigate for anyone unfamiliar with the terrain.

About two miles further up the trail, Cooper and Harley started barking frantically as they stood close to the edge of the trail where it dropped off.

Aiden glanced over at Zach who nodded in return, and both men began running as Zach announced over the radio, "Dispatch this is K-9 1, we've got a possible location for the missing hiker."

A female voice belonging to Deanna Harper, the Clear Mountain police dispatcher replied, "Copy that, K-9 1, what's your location? What's the status of the hiker?"

Both men reached the side of the trail where the pair of dogs were barking, intent on something below them, drawing both officers' gaze below.

On a small jetty of the cliff—halfway down the ravine—Aiden could make out a form crumpled against the edge of the mountain.

"Dispatch, we have a confirmed sighting of the hiker," Zach stated over the radio. "Be advised, hiker is located halfway down Whisper Ravine. We're going to need the air unit's assistance at our position, three clicks north of Meadow Ridge. I'm lighting up a flare now for location identification."

"What's the status of the hiker, K-9 1?"

"Dispatch, the status is unknown at this time," Zach said cautiously.

"Mr. Williams, can you hear me?" Aiden shouted down. "I'm Officer O'Connell with Clear Mountain Search and Rescue."

A few seconds later, a male voice filled with a

mixture of fear and relief, shouted back up, "Yes, I can hear you. Please, can you get me out of here?"

"How are you doing, Mr. Williams?" Aiden inquired.

"Not good, I cut my leg when I fell down the ravine. I've managed to keep the bleeding under control, but when I heard the barking, I jerked against the cliff, causing the wound to re-open. It's bleeding heavily now."

"How are you feeling?" Aiden asked, trying to assess the hiker's condition.

"I'm feeling woozy, like I might pass out at any moment."

Aiden knew what that meant; the hiker only had a few minutes before he would lose consciousness from blood loss and then succumb to the injury. Aiden wasn't going to let that happen.

Shrugging his pack off his back, Aiden placed it down on the ground, then opened it up and reached inside to pull out a rope.

"What are you doing?" Zach asked Aiden with suspicion. "You know protocol. We're supposed to wait until the air unit arrives to assist us."

Aiden shook his head and said in a lowered tone, "This guy can't wait that long. I need to get down to him now."

Handing Zach the rope, he ordered, "Tie off the

end and help guide me down." Aiden secured the rope around his waist and then placed his pack back on.

"I should probably argue with you about this course of action, but after working with you the past year, I know how useless it would be."

"Good, you can save us both the trouble."

A few minutes later, Aiden was rappelling down the side of Whisper Ravine, making sure to keep a fast but steady rhythm as Zach spotted his descent from the top.

As Aiden's feet touched the ledge of the cliff, he heard Mr. Williams' state in a nervous tone, "I didn't think anyone would find me in time."

"I need you to remain calm, Mr. Williams, while I see what I can do about your wound."

Aiden pulled his pack free once more and opened it up, extracting a medical kit. Setting it down next to Mr. Williams, he moved into a crouching position next to the hiker. After opening the kit, Aiden pulled out a pair of gloves and put them on.

Reaching out, he lifted Mr. Williams' hand, but even the momentary removal of pressure caused the bandana to seep through with blood. Aiden realized there was no way he could remove the makeshift bandage safely.

"I'm going to need to leave your bandana in place

and wrap it with this," he said, as he held up a roll of gauze. "The extra pressure should help keep the bleeding under control."

Mr. Williams nodded and allowed Aiden to work on his leg.

After securing the bandage, Aiden said over the radio, "Dispatch this is K-9 2, I'm with the hiker. I just secured his wound and we're ready for transport by the air unit."

"K-9 2, what are you doing with that hiker?" Aiden immediately recognized the angry, deep, male voice of his lieutenant coming over the radio.

Avoiding answering directly in front of the hiker and risking upsetting the man, Aiden stated, "I'll explain why there wasn't another option when I get back to the station, L.T."

"You bet your bottom dollar, you will," the gruff voice commanded.

"Did I get you in trouble?" Mr. Williams asked.

"No, of course not. L.T. is always like that," Aiden stated with a grin. "It's his job to watch out for his men."

The whipping sound of the helicopter's blades drew Aiden and Mr. Williams' attention to the south of them. As the red and white air unit approached the ledge, Aiden heard over the radio, "Clear Mountain Search and Rescue, this is the Boulder County Air Unit. We hear you're in need of our assistance."

Aiden replied back, "Boulder County Air, this is K-9 2, it's good to see you. I have two for transport. Can you send down the rescue basket?"

"Got you covered, K-9 2, get ready to receive."

A few moments later, a red basket attached to a cable was lowered down to them along with a secondary line for Aiden.

"I'm going to help you get into this basket and secure you. I will then attach myself so I can ride up with you and keep you stable as they pull us up."

Mr. Williams' eyes grew wide with fright. "How safe is this?"

"Safer than staying here on this ledge," Aiden assured. "It's okay, you've got nothing to worry about. I'll make sure you arrive back to your wife in one piece."

With a nod, Mr. Williams allowed Aiden to help him into the rescue basket. Then Aiden secured himself alongside.

"Boulder County Air, we're ready to ascend."

"Copy, K-9 2, bringing you up now."

Aiden held onto the rescue bucket and made sure to keep it level as they were pulled up and brought on board the helicopter. Once Aiden handed off the hiker to the other officers in the unit, he secured himself in a seat.

As he looked out the window, Aiden noticed that the other three Clear Mountain Search and Rescue officers and sergeant were standing next to Zach and the dogs.

"K-9 1, this is K-9 2, I'll see you back at the station," Aiden stated over the radio. "Take good care of Cooper for me, will you?"

"You bet, K-9 2, see you soon."

TWO

Lindsay Wright received the call from her supervisor to check on the welfare of a child. A report from a local school stated the child had excessive bug bites covering her body and complained of not having food in the home. As Lindsay approached the rundown house, she hoped the allegations were incorrect. However, when she saw the condition of the house, her heart lurched in pity.

Though common in the rural parts of Boulder County to find sub-par living conditions, most families did their best. The county worked with them to fix their problems rather than remove a child from their home; however, there were limits. Such as in the case when there were animal feces and bugs covering the floor of a dwelling and no food was in the fridge or cabinets. Couple this with bug bites covering a little girl's body, and Lindsay knew the child couldn't stay in the home.

As Lindsay talked with the mother, she smelled alcohol on the woman's breath and worried she might become combative. Lindsay decided she needed police presence in order to help with the removal of the child. Not wanting to tip off the mother about what was going to happen, Lindsay stepped out of the dwelling—still remaining within sight of the mother and daughter—and called the local sheriff's office.

Once the deputy arrived, Lindsay had the difficult job of informing the mother. "Mrs. Burgess, I'm required to take Mandy now."

"What kind of a monster are you?" Mrs. Burgess accused as she held her daughter in her arms. "Only a completely heartless person could rip a child from her mother's arms."

"I'm sorry, ma'am, but Mandy can't stay in these living conditions," Lindsay explained. "It's not safe for her here."

"You think you got the right to judge me?" the indignant woman railed at Lindsay. "I work hard and try my best, but I don't have time to keep up on everything since Mandy's no-good father ran off on us."

"Ma'am, I understand you're in a difficult situation," Lindsay sympathized, "but my hands are tied."

The deputy had to hold back the mother and keep her inside as Lindsay took the child out of the house.

As Lindsay buckled the crying child into the carseat, she whispered "Shhh, Mandy, it's going to be alright," trying to assure her. "I'm taking you to a safe place to stay while all of this is worked out."

Lindsay snapped the seatbelt buckle into place, but as her hand grazed the side of the little girl's leg, the child flinched, crying out in pain.

"What's wrong sweetie?" Lindsay asked.

"I have a boo-boo," the tow-headed child said, pointing to her leg.

Lindsay leaned forward causing her blond hair to fall into her face. She brushed the locks out of her face. Gingerly, she folded up the edge of the right leg of the shorts and inhaled sharply. Tears filled her green eyes as she saw the giant infected bite on the girl's inner thigh. Why hadn't her mother done something about this?

Lindsay couldn't leave the bite in its current condition. After taking a quick picture for documentation, she went around to the back of her Chevy

Traverse, opened the back hatch, and pulled out a medical supply kit.

She came back around and opened the kit, pulling out a wipe and bandage. She wanted to put ointment on the wound, but not knowing if the child was allergic to anything, she refrained.

After giving Mandy a bear to play with on the car ride back to Clear Mountain, Lindsay concentrated on the next step of getting the child somewhere safe.

Even after being a social worker for over two years, Lindsay still found it hard to deal with the difficult situations she saw on a daily basis. Silently, Lindsay sent up a prayer asking God to give her strength and to help her find a good placement for the little girl. Lindsay knew God had given her a purpose to help children like Mandy and she wasn't going to give up following the path God called her to walk.

THREE

The furious look on Lieutenant Davis' face as Aiden walked through the door of the station almost made him turn around and head back out. Aiden, however, knew he was going to have to face the consequences for his actions at some point; it might as well be now.

"What were you thinking, rappelling down that ravine like you did? You know that's not what protocol dictates."

"I know L.T., but if I had followed protocol, that hiker would have died on that ledge waiting for the air unit to arrive."

Crossing his arms, Lieutenant Davis stared at Aiden for several seconds before stating, "You have a point, but officially, I have to give you a verbal warning not to disobey protocol again. Take this seriously, Aiden, or I will have to give you your first written reprimand."

As Zach entered the room and snorted, he stated sarcastically, "Oh, no, we wouldn't want the face of the Clear Mountain police to go and tarnish his otherwise exemplary reputation, now would we."

Lieutenant Davis' eyes narrowed and snapped to Zach. "As opposed to your less than stellar one?"

With a shrug, Zach replied, "Can I help that I was born with a rebel spirit and the simplicity of this place makes me want to revolt?"

Clear Mountain police substation was a small department, so when there was no need for an officer's specialty, officers were assigned to routine calls for service. The K-9 unit was no exception. Both of the Clear Mountain Police dogs were multi-purpose trained, meaning they were able to work assignments from search and rescue, to bomb detection, to narcotics.

Yet, even though they were trained to handle any number of problems, most of the 9-1-1 calls were docile due to the area. The often-monotonous calls made Zach act out in an effort to inject some excitement into their shifts.

"You're lucky I'm not in the mood to train another officer, Zach, or I would have a good mind to toss your rebel spirit out on its rear." In an admonishing tone, Lieutenant Davis added, "You're already on thin ice due to the Wimble bomb threat incident."

The incident their supervisor was referring to was when Mrs. Wimble—one of Clear Mountain's elderly residents who didn't always have the sanest frame of reference—called for the third time in a row claiming someone had placed a bomb in the engine of her car.

Zach and Harley were assigned the call, and when they arrived, he had Harley inspect the vehicle. When she found no trace of a bomb, Zach informed Mrs. Wimble she was mistaken about her fears.

The woman wouldn't accept his explanation and insisted he was wrong. To prove his point, he hopped into the car and drove it around the block to show her it wouldn't blow up. The woman was irate and called Lieutenant Davis to tell him about the incident. The rash choice earned Zach a written reprimand and a warning that if he did anything like that again, he would face a suspension.

"Both of your shifts are over. I'll see you back here at 0800 hours," Lieutenant Davis stated in a dismissive tone.

Aiden and Zach knew not to argue with their boss. Turning around, the men left the station without a word.

Near Aiden's car stood a curvy brunette wearing

a skin tight red suit with a skirt just long enough and a shirt just high enough to be considered professional. The outfit left very little to the imagination and Aiden felt awkward, not wanting to let his eyes linger too long on the familiar woman.

"What are you doing here, Miss Watts?" Aiden said, purposely not making eye contact with the newspaper reporter.

"I heard there was a hiker who went missing and you made a daring rescue to save him. Care to comment?" Natalie asked, pushing out her voice recorder towards him.

"Like I've told you before, Miss Watts, I was just doing my job," Aiden stated, trying to hide the irritation in his voice.

"You don't want to give me a quote?" she said with a pouty voice. "If you need more time, we could go get a drink and I could interview you over at The Lucky Penny."

Of course, she would want to take him to The Lucky Penny. It was where all the cops hung out after work and where all the badge bunnies frequented to land a date. He had spent his fair share of nights at the bar, but tonight he was exhausted and not in the mood to fend off unwanted attention. How could he get out of this?

She must have noticed his hesitation because she

immediately switched tactics, saying, "I guess if you can't give me a quote, I could always go speak with Lieutenant Davis about the rescue and let him know you didn't feel up to letting me interview you."

He had already ticked off Lieutenant Davis once tonight; he didn't want to repeat the same mistake by being the reason this woman went inside and badgered him. Giving in, he stated, "Fine, I guess I can go over to The Lucky Penny for a few minutes."

A sultry smile curved the woman's mouth before she said, "I'll follow you over in my car."

FOUR

After the day she'd had, the last thing Lindsay wanted to do was go on the blind date from the website her best friend and roommate, Erica, signed her up on. Granted, it was a Christian dating website, but still, Lindsay always thought she would meet her future husband in the old-fashioned way by running into him somewhere and having an instant connection.

When the serendipitous moment never happened, Lindsay decided to give up on dating and focus on her career; that was until Erica informed her last week she had signed her up for a Christian dating site. Lindsay wasn't sure if she would ever get used to the new way of dating; it seemed so cold and impersonal.

Looking at herself one final time in the mirror, Lindsay tucked the few rogue strands of blond hair behind her ears before turning around to face Erica.

"You look so pretty in that emerald dress," Erica stated with a smile. "It enhances the greenness of your eyes. Bill is going to be knocked over when he sees you."

"Thanks, Erica, I just wish I wasn't so tired. Today was exhausting."

"Yes, but that's why it's so great you are going out. It will take your mind off of all that."

Although Erica was a good friend, she often didn't understand why Lindsay couldn't leave her work at the office. Erica worked as a dental assistant, so her job didn't take an emotional toll like Lindsay's did. It wasn't that Lindsay didn't want to have a life outside her job, it was that her heart couldn't keep from worrying about the kids on her case load.

"I guess you're right. It'll be nice to focus on something else for a while," Lindsay conceded. Then, remembering what she would be doing, she added with apprehension, "even if it means spending a couple of awkward hours with a total stranger over dinner."

"That's the spirit," Erica said in jest. Her laughter caused her brown bob to shake before she added, "Go get him, Cowgirl."

Lindsay smirked at the nickname from high school. Being raised on a ranch outside Clear Mountain, the kids from town gave her the nickname when she arrived the first day of freshmen year in Wranglers and boots.

Though her wardrobe had changed over the years, often being caught in a pair of slacks with a matching blouse because of work, she was still a rancher's daughter at heart. She enjoyed the outdoors when she had the time.

"Don't forget to call me at exactly nine," Lindsay reminded Erica. "If things get weird, I don't want to stay there any longer than I have to."

Grabbing her purse and coat, Lindsay headed out the door.

As she sat on one of the benches in the waiting area for the restaurant, Lindsay glanced at her phone: ten past eight. Bill was already late; she wondered how long she needed to wait before she could leave. Erica would be upset if she found out Lindsay left and didn't give Bill a chance. Even though Lindsay could leave and go to the movies, it would require her to lie when Erica asked her how it went. Lindsay prided herself on being an honest person, knowing even when no one else knew she lied, God did.

A short, balding man was making a beeline directly for her. Lindsay was confused as the man looked nothing like the photo on the profile for Bill.

"Wow, you actually look exactly like your picture, down to the freckle under your right eye," the stout man stated with an eager grin.

"I'm sorry, do you have me confused with someone else?" Lindsay asked, still bewildered. "I'm supposed to be meeting someone here tonight, but I don't think—"

Cutting her off, the man interjected, "I'm Bill. You're supposed to be meeting me."

Lindsay's eyebrows shot up in surprise. What was going on? The man in front of her looked nothing like the man from the online profile.

Bill must have noticed her reaction because he quickly stated, "That picture was of me from ten years ago when I was in high school."

Doing the math in her head, Lindsay quickly realized he had lied about his age as well. They were both supposed to be in their mid-twenties, but that made him a few years older than her.

Even though his lies were a red flag, Lindsay had been raised to give people the benefit of the doubt, so she simply asked, "Is there a reason you used such an old photo and put a different age?"

Bill's eyes fell to the ground as he asked, "Would you have come if I had used a more recent photo or put my age?"

Lindsay wanted to say yes, but the truth was, he was probably right, she would have skipped right over him. Feeling embarrassed for her judgmental nature, Lindsay offered, "I think our table is ready. Should we go sit down?"

"You're staying?" he asked in disbelief.

As soon as she nodded, Bill turned and asked the hostess, "Can you seat us now?"

A few minutes later, they were seated at a two-person table with menus in hand. As they perused the offerings, the awkward silence mushroomed out.

The server appeared to take their order, but before Lindsay could speak, Bill said, "We'll take a bottle of your house red wine. We'll also both have the steak, medium rare with baked potatoes."

Lindsay had to force her mouth to keep from dropping open in shock. Never in all her life had someone ordered for her without asking her what she wanted. What was this man doing? Did he live in the dark ages when women had no thoughts of their own?

Before the server could leave, Lindsay stopped

the woman with her voice, "Can you please change my order to the house salad with the salmon fillet? And I would also like a glass of iced tea."

The server gave Lindsay a sympathetic look before scribbling down the change in the order.

"You said you were a huge fan of red wine on your profile," he accused.

"I think you have me confused with someone else," Lindsay stated clearly. "I rarely drink, and never when I have to drive home later."

His eyes narrowed for a moment before he asked in annoyance, "Let me guess, you don't eat red meat either?"

Lindsay shook her head. "I have nothing against meat; I just wanted to have a salad."

He glanced at her figure. "You've got an amazing body; not sure why you think you need to diet."

Did she just hear him correctly? What was wrong with this man?

Lindsay resisted the urge to pick up her phone and look at the time. It didn't matter anyway as she knew forty-five minutes had not passed yet, and Erica wouldn't be calling any time soon.

After sending up a silent prayer for strength, Lindsay was grateful when her iced tea and some rolls arrived at the table, giving her a welcomed distraction from Bill's gawking at her.

"You said on your profile you're a social worker. You plan on quitting once you start a family?"

Lindsay's eyes darted up to meet Bill's. From his profile, she hadn't pegged him for the traditional patriarchal type. It wasn't that she was opposed to staying home with the kids—being a stay-at-home-mom was one of the most wonderful jobs in the world—it was simply that she wasn't sure she could have children. None of that, however, was this man's business, and she refused to discuss such a personal part of her life with him.

"I will do whatever God tells me to do," she said instead.

With a shrug, Bill stated, "I don't think it works that way. God doesn't just come out and tell you what to do. You have to think for yourself. I thought since you were an 'educated' woman, you would be smart enough to know that."

Fed up with this man's obnoxiously condescending behavior, Lindsay stood up and threw her napkin on the table. Picking up her purse, she dug out two twenties from her wallet and threw them on the table.

"I think it's quite clear this isn't going to work. I've had a rough day, and I can't sit through anymore of this."

Without waiting for a response from Bill, Lindsay

headed towards the door of the restaurant, vowing to take down her dating profile as soon as she got home. If this was the type of men who were out there, she would rather be single.

Pushing the door open, she turned to the left and headed down the sidewalk towards her parked car. The wind was blowing hard, causing Lindsay to keep her head tucked down.

Suddenly, she bumped into something hard. Her eyes flew up to meet the most gorgeous set of chocolate pools she had ever encountered. Stepping back, she took in the rest of the man.

He was tall with broad shoulders, and though his brown hair was cut short, she could see the tips were sun-kissed blond on the ends. He was wearing a black leather coat with a white shirt and blue jeans, and from his demeanor, she could tell he was confident, but didn't present as vain.

"Are you alright?" he asked her.

"Yes, I'm fine," she said. "I just wasn't paying attention. The chill from the wind caused me to rush to my car."

With a dazzling smile, he said, "It's pretty cold out tonight. It's probably going to reach freezing temperatures, so we might get snow for the first time this year."

"I love the first snow," they both said at the same time.

With a chuckle, the stranger said, "Great minds think alike." Holding out his hand, he added, "I'm Aiden O'Connell."

Taking his hand in her own, she greeted in return, "I'm Lindsay Wright."

"It's nice to meet you, Lindsay. Maybe you should—"

Before the hunky guy could finish his sentence, the door beside them burst open and another man came stumbling out.

"There you are, Aiden. I was looking for you," the other man slurred out as he leaned on his friend. Glancing over at Lindsay, he raised an eyebrow and asked, "Who's this?"

"I'd introduce you, Zach, but you won't remember in the morning anyway." Looking over at her, Aiden added, "I'm sorry about this. Apparently, things didn't go too well in there for him. He's my partner, and I need to be getting him home."

Partner? A sudden sinking sensation of disappointment crashed over Lindsay as she watched the good-looking—apparently unavailable—man walk away.

Pulling the collar of her coat up around her neck, the door next to her swung open a second time, and a pretty brunette came out, asking in a slightly slurred voice, "Did you see a tall, brown-haired fella out here?"

"I think you just missed him. He said he needed to help his *partner* get home."

"That's so like Aiden. He's always on duty." With a heavy sigh, the other woman confessed, "I've been chasing that badge for two months now and haven't gotten anywhere. I'm not sure what it's going to take."

The woman stumbled a bit as she pulled open the door and sauntered back inside the bar.

Badge? The new information clicked into place. *Officer* Aiden O'Connell had been mentioned on the news and in the papers, several times over the past year for heroic feats. He was a highly decorated officer who had transferred from Boulder.

As Lindsay reached her car, thoughts of the handsome police officer danced in her mind. She wondered if she had finally just had her serendipitous moment?

FIVE

Aiden and Zach started to head towards the police substation's front doors with Cooper and Harley on their leashes.

"Have a good lunch, guys," Deanna shouted out after them.

The men turned around and watched as the buxom red-head took off her headset and patted her curls back into place. Being the only source of feminine charm in the Clear Mountain substation, most of the officers fawned all over her. Though there were many female police officers in Boulder County, the small town remained completely comprised of male cops.

"Thanks, Deanna," Aiden said.

"Care to join us?" Zach offered with a flirtatious grin.

Shaking her head, she replied, "No, I've got too much paperwork to catch up on."

Having the dual task of being the lone dispatcher and assistant to Captain McGregor, she often only had time to eat lunch at her desk. Aiden also suspected she was avoiding a social setting with Zach. At every available opportunity, he made a pass at her. She, in turn, had made it clear she was uninterested.

"Your loss," Zach stated, running his hand through his black hair, before turning around and heading out the door with Aiden following behind.

The men loaded up both Cooper and Harley into the kennels in the back of the police SUV, knowing they could be assigned a call at a moment's notice.

A few minutes later, they pulled up in front of Happy's Burgers. Jumping out of the SUV, Aiden waited for Zach to lock the vehicle with a second set of keys. They needed to leave the engine running with the AC on for the dogs in the back.

After making their way into the restaurant, the men ordered their food. The clerk smiled at them saying, "The food is on the house, Officers."

"Thank you, ma'am," Aiden said, pulling out a five and placing it in the tip jar.

Finding a corner table near the window where they could watch the SUV, the men sat down to eat.

As they were finishing up their meal, Zach stated, "You know, I still can't believe you didn't close the deal with Natalie Watts the other night. She was all over you and you just brushed her off."

Sighing, Aiden explained, "She doesn't care about me; she never even asked me a single question about my personal life. I'm tired of wasting my time on meaningless one-night-stands. I want to find someone interested in sharing a life with me, and if I can't find that, I just want to concentrate on testing well on the sergeant exam at the end of the year."

"Man, you're all work and no play," Zach scolded in a teasing manner as he took a drink of his soda, then continued, "I need a wingman, not a stick-in-the-mud."

Glancing around the room, Zach gestured with his head to a blond woman sitting at a nearby booth. "For example, did you even see the hot blond sitting over there? I bet if you approached her, she would jump at the chance to go on a date with you."

Aiden's eyes followed in the direction of Zach's gesture. The back of a curvy blond woman was towards them. She was sitting across from a little boy who looked to be about six-years-old.

"She's got a kid, Zach, which means she's probably married."

With a shrug, Zach replied, "Means less complications, if you know what I mean."

Aiden knew exactly what Zach meant; a husband never stopped him from hitting on a woman, but it was a no-go for Aiden. He might not go to church currently, but the influence of his Christian upbringing ran deep.

"I got to go drain the lizard," Zach said with a smirk. "Why don't you surprise me and go ask out that hot mom over there?"

Something seemed familiar about the woman, but there was no way he was going over there. "Thanks, but I'm good just concentrating on work," Aiden said to the retreating figure of his partner.

SIX

As she sat across from one of the first kids she had been assigned to take care of, Lindsay's heart filled with sadness. She wanted nothing more than to erase the dejected look from Alex Sterling's face.

Up until a week ago, Alex had been in a loving and supportive foster home until the father's work had forced an immediate transfer. The sudden move by the foster parents left Alex displaced.

Currently, the seven-year-old boy was staying at a shelter group home until Lindsay could find him another foster placement. The situation was less than ideal since he needed a permanent home and getting attached to a temporary caregiver would only cause more trauma for him.

"Are you still having problems with the older boys in the home?" Lindsay asked.

Keeping his eyes averted, he shrugged. "Nothing I can't handle."

"You don't have to pretend for me, Alex," Lindsay coaxed. "It's okay to tell me if something is going on. I can go talk to the boys that are causing the problem."

Lindsay had heard from one of her other kids who was staying in the shelter group home that some of the bigger boys were picking on Alex due to his small stature. Alex's mother had been a drug addict while she was pregnant with Alex. This caused him to be underweight for his age, a fact that Lindsay could see caused Alex to feel inferior.

His frightened eyes darted up to meet hers before he masked the fear. "I told you, nothing's the matter. Can we just go?"

With a nod, Lindsay scooted out of the booth and waited for Alex to do the same.

As they started to walk down the aisle, a smile sprung to Alex's face as he pointed and shouted, "Look, a K-9 officer."

Without waiting for Lindsay to respond, Alex rushed over to the officer's side and started talking to him.

Lindsay's eyes grew round with recognition as

she took in the handsome figure of Officer Aiden O'Connell. Although his uniform had his name and position stitched above the pockets of both sides of his chest, she would have remembered him without any help.

"Can I see your dog?" she heard Alex asking Aiden.

Standing up, Aiden grabbed his tray and moved towards the trash can behind him. "Sure. I can take you to see him. I was just finishing up anyway."

Lindsay stepped forward, excusing Alex's interruption. "I'm sorry, Officer O'Connell. Alex just loves police officers and wants to be a K-9 handler when he grows up. I hope he's not bothering you."

"It's no problem," Aiden assured her. "Like I said, I was already finished." Giving her a friendly smile that made his eyes shine, he added, "It's good to see you again."

"You too," she said as she felt herself blush under his watchful stare.

"Where's your dog?" Alex asked.

"Cooper's in my vehicle along with our other K-9, Harley."

"You can just leave them out in the car?" the boy asked with incredulity.

"We have two sets of keys, so we can leave the

vehicle locked with the AC running to keep them comfortable."

"Don't they get lonely?"

With a chuckle, Aiden explained, "We don't leave them in there too long. Besides, they have each other." Glancing behind them, Aiden said, "I need to get the other set of keys from my partner. I'll be right back."

A few minutes later, Aiden appeared with a set of keys in hand. As he headed towards the door, Aiden said over his shoulder, "Follow me."

SEVEN

Lindsay and Alex trailed after Aiden as he walked over to the police SUV. As he opened the back hatch, two dogs came to attention and looked at Aiden expectantly through their kennels.

"Hold on just a minute, Cooper, while I get your leash," Aiden said with audible affection in his voice. The devoted look in the larger dog's eyes showed the undeniable connection between handler and K-9.

After undoing the latch to the cage, Aiden hooked the leash onto the collar of Cooper.

"That's a good boy, Cooper," Aiden said as he rubbed the ears of the German Shepherd while stealing a glance out of the corner of his eyes at Lindsay Wright. She looked pretty in her black slacks and cream blouse, but not in the trying-too-hard sort of way.

"Can I pet him?" Alex asked.

"Give me a moment," Aiden said as he stepped back and let Cooper jump down from the back of the SUV while controlling him with the leash. Aiden guided Cooper over to some nearby grass and handed the dog his chew toy.

Kneeling down beside him, he continued to keep his hand on Cooper's collar as he said to Alex, "You can come over now and pet him."

With a giant smile on his face, Alex slowly approached Cooper, bending down on the other side of the dog. Cautiously, he reached out and placed his hand on his back and began to lightly stroke his fur.

"Why does he have to keep that chew toy in his mouth?" Alex inquired.

Lindsay came over to join them and said apologetically, "Alex tends to ask a lot of questions. He's an inquisitive kid."

With a lopsided grin directed at Lindsay, Aiden stated, "It doesn't bother me. I enjoy answering questions about Cooper." Looking at Alex, he added, "Asking questions is a sign of intelligence after all." Answering the boy's inquiry, Aiden stated, "Police dogs have two modes: work and social. The chew toy tells Cooper it's social time."

Nodding his head, Alex replied, "Makes sense. I can see he's relaxed."

From behind them, Aiden heard Zach say, "Don't let him fool you; Cooper can flip from social to work mode in a second. All police dogs can, which is why you have to know how to handle them properly."

Everyone's attention shifted to Zach for a moment as he got Harley out of her kennel, then brought her over to the grass near Cooper. Handing over her own chew toy, Zach said, "This is Harley."

Alex turned his attention to the other dog and started to pet her next. Aiden stood up and gave Cooper the signal to heel with the leash on as he moved closer to Lindsay.

"He seems like a bright boy," Aiden said. "You must be proud of him."

"He's come a long way since—"

Before Lindsay could finish, Deanna came over the radio saying, "K-9 1 & 2, we have a disturbance at the thrift store on 3rd Street. We need you to follow up on it."

Aiden pushed the button on his receiver and said, "Dispatch, this is K-9 2, show us en route." He then turned to Lindsay, saying, "I'm sorry. I wish we could stay longer since Alex seems to be enjoying spending time with the dogs."

Harley pawed Alex gently and Lindsay said, "It seems to go both ways."

Zach stood up and brought Harley to her kennel, loading her inside before saying, "We got to go, Aiden."

"It was nice seeing you again, ma'am."

She cringed at the formal address. "Please, don't refer to me as ma'am. I'm far too young for that to be happening. You can call me Lindsay."

"I can do that," he stated with a smile, "which means you need to call me Aiden."

The conversation was easy with Lindsay. For the first time since his breakup with Veronica, he felt like there might be a reason to start dating again.

"Come on, Alex. We need to let the nice officers go," Lindsay said as she held out her hand to him. "They have work to do."

Aiden couldn't help but notice the gold band with two hearts on her left ring finger, glinting in the sunlight. His hopeful cheer vanished, replaced by disappointment at the realization that Lindsay must be married. When he had first seen her with Alex, he knew it was a possibility, but he hoped the boy was her nephew or perhaps she was a single mother. The ring confirmed the worst possibility; she was spoken for.

He didn't know why it bothered him so much to

think of Lindsay being unavailable, but it did. He should be focusing on his career and making sergeant, not on some random woman he'd run into, even if it had been twice now.

Once Cooper was secured in his kennel, Aiden hopped up into the SUV next to Zach who was already in the driver's seat. He watched in the rearview mirror as the beautiful blond waved goodbye and a pang of regret filled the pit of his stomach.

EIGHT

As Aiden drove off, Lindsay couldn't help but wonder about him. Was he married? She didn't see a ring, but she wasn't naive enough to think all married men wore one. Some left them off for safety reasons and others for more nefarious purposes. She didn't get the sense Aiden was that type of man—although his fellow officer was a different story. She had seen him blatantly checking her out several times. If Aiden wasn't married, did he have a girlfriend? Did he want one? If he was that gentle with his dog, would he be the same way with a woman?

Chastising herself for letting her mind go there, Lindsay tried to focus on anything else as she drove Alex back to the shelter group home. Yet, no matter how hard she tried, she couldn't keep from thinking about the friendly cop.

She wanted to blame Aiden's good looks for her focus on him, but her attraction to him went deeper than just appearance. His friendly disposition and kindness with Alex made her think there was potential for a relationship.

Lindsay's last boyfriend, Rick, popped into her head, reminding her why she was so opposed to dating. Rick had seemed great in the beginning too, until he broke her heart.

A chill ran up Lindsay's back as she sat on the medical exam table in her gynecologist's office and waited to hear what the future held for her. When the doctor returned, she would either find out she could have children or her dreams would be crushed.

Before her mother died of cancer when she was ten, Lindsay used to ask why she didn't have any brothers or sisters. Her mother told her she was a miracle, and she was lucky to even have her. Lindsay hadn't thought about babies until Rick started talking about marriage and children, prompting her to wonder if she could have children of her own.

"Good afternoon, Lindsay," Doctor Roberts said as he entered the room.

As her eyes met his, she knew the news wasn't good. "I'm sorry to tell you, but you have advanced endometriosis."

"Is there anything I can do? I think I heard somewhere that surgery can help."

Shaking his head, Doctor Roberts said solemnly, "It won't work in your case. It's highly unlikely you will ever be able to carry a successful pregnancy."

Lindsay left the doctor's office dejected. How could she tell Rick? What would he think? She felt inadequate and worried he wouldn't look at her in the same way.

As she knocked on the door to Rick's apartment, she inhaled deeply, then held the breath in place.

Rick looked good wearing a pair of sweats and t-shirt as he leaned against the frame of the door. "What are you doing here? I wasn't expecting you until tonight."

"We need to talk," Lindsay said as she glided past him and into his living room.

"What's up?" he asked casually.

Sitting down on the couch, she placed her hands in her lap and gripped them tight in apprehension.

"I was at the doctor's office earlier today—" He sat next to her and waited for her to continue. "And it wasn't good news."

He placed his hand on top of hers and asked, "What's the matter?"

She tried to swallow the lump in her throat before saying, "I have endometriosis."

His brows came together in a furrow. "I don't understand. What does that mean?"

She let out a deep breath, then whispered as her eyes dropped to the floor, "I can't have children."

Rick yanked his hand back as if she were on fire. "What are you talking about? You're young and in great shape."

"It's true that both of those play a factor in fertility, but my diagnosis is certain. My mother had fertility issues, but honestly, I didn't think about it until we became serious."

Rick started to pace the room in an angry stalking motion. "You've known the whole time we've been together and you're just now telling me? How could you let me get so serious with you and not say something?"

She jumped up and moved over to him. Placing her hand on his arm, she pleaded, "We can still have a family. There's always adoption."

He pulled away from her. "I want my own children to raise, not someone else's."

"Maybe you will feel differently after a few weeks," she countered. "I know it's a lot to take in, but you just need to give it some time and pray about it."

Shaking his head, he stated firmly, "I won't change my mind on this."

She spent the next six months beating herself up over the fact she couldn't give Rick what he wanted.

She finished her degree and threw herself into her new job as a social worker.

A year later, she found out Rick was married and expecting his first child. She had dated sporadically up until then, but the news hit her like a ton of bricks. She had given up on dating until Erica set up her profile.

Although Aiden's good looks and easy disposition were enticing, she didn't know if she could go through something like that again.

Besides, she was too busy with her job, wasn't she? She didn't have time for a serious boyfriend. It wasn't like she was going to be seeing him again, so it didn't matter anyway.

"Those officers sure were nice and their dogs were awesome," Alex said from the backseat of her car.

"Yes, it was great of them to let us meet Cooper and Harley."

"Do you think we will see them again?" Alex asked.

"You never know," Lindsay replied, "it depends what God has planned."

NINE

Aiden pulled his police SUV through the gates of the Clear Mountain Elementary School parking his vehicle at the end of the carnival area.

Rows of booths for games lined one area along with vendors set up for food; all of them were decorated with either Christmas or winter themes.

Just like the past five years, the school had asked the police department to come and talk with families. Lieutenant Davis had assigned the K-9 units to attend knowing they would be a good fit as the face of the department for the community outreach.

Zach parked his own vehicle next to Aiden's, both of them opening the doors and hatch for the kids to be able to see inside the vehicles. Next, they pulled the dogs out of their kennels bringing them to a heel on their leashes.

"You ready for this?" Zach asked Aiden. "It's your first time doing one of these outreach events at a school. The constant onslaught of people can be brutal, especially when kids are involved."

"I think I can handle whatever happens," Aiden countered. "Besides, I like kids."

"Don't say I didn't warn you."

Glancing down at his watch, Aiden realized the students and their families would be arriving any moment. Taking a wide stance, Aiden prepared himself for the rush of kids who would want to see Cooper and ask questions.

A few minutes later, children lined up to speak to Aiden and Zach about being cops, and to look through the patrol vehicles. A few of them asked to pet the dogs while the parents watched and occasionally thanked them for their service.

The steady stream of children didn't relent. After some time passed, he realized Zach was correct. He was beginning to feel the strain of the steady barrage. Rubbing his hand on the back of his neck, he stretched for a moment while there was a break in gathered students. Glancing down, he made sure Cooper wasn't stressed out. His wagging tail and light panting made it clear he was content for the time being.

Off in the distance, he heard a little boy shout in excitement, "Look, there's Officer Aiden and Cooper."

Aiden turned towards the direction of the voice and found Alex running towards him with Lindsay following behind.

TEN

In the distance, Lindsay saw Aiden standing with Cooper next to his police SUV. He looked handsome in his dark blue uniform with his polished badge shining in the light and his inviting smile beckoning her to come closer.

"Hi, Officer Aiden. It's so cool you're here at my school carnival," Alex exclaimed. "I've been telling all my friends about how awesome Cooper is and now they can see for themselves."

Aiden nodded. "They sure can. When you get a chance, you should bring them over."

Bending down next to Cooper, Alex asked, "Can I pet Cooper?"

"Sure, Champ, just make sure to be gentle like you were last time."

Aiden turned his attention to Lindsay and stated, "We never did get that snow, but they're calling for it tonight."

Lindsay's eyebrows shot up in shock. "I'm surprised you remember the details of our conversation from the night we met. Most of the men I know can't remember what happened two hours ago, let alone two weeks."

Tapping the side of his head, Aiden explained, "Details are everything for a cop. We have to remember Miranda rights, the facts of cases, the penal code, so even when we aren't at work, it spills into our personal life."

Lindsay smiled and said, "I kind of have to do the same thing for my job. My cases—"

Before she could finish telling him about her job, Alex interrupted saying, "I'm hungry. Can I go get a hot dog?"

"You can have one hot dog meal," Lindsay instructed as she opened her purse and pulled out a five-dollar bill, then handed it over to Alex.

"Can I get a cookie too?" he asked with pleading eyes.

Pausing for a moment, Lindsay pulled out another dollar and said, "Okay, but only one. I don't want you getting all hyped up on sugar."

With a toothy grin, Alex said, "Thank you,"

before rushing off towards the food vendors.

With an appreciative tone, Aiden said, "You're a great mom."

A fit of laughter burst out of Lindsay. It took her several seconds before she could speak. "I'm not Alex's mother. I'm his social worker."

Aiden chuckled. "Sorry about that. I just assumed he was your kid."

"It kind of feels that way. I've had Alex since I first became a social worker two years ago. He was one of the first kids assigned to me." With a hint of sadness, she added, "He's had a rough life."

"How did you end up bringing him here tonight? Don't foster parents usually bring them to events like this?" Aiden probed.

"Alex is between foster parents right now," Lindsay explained. "He's in a shelter group home until I can find him a permanent placement."

"That's a bummer. He seems like a good kid."

"He is, which is why when he asked me if I would bring him to the carnival, I agreed."

"Sounds like Alex—"

"Hey guys, sorry I have to interrupt," Zach said, "but the line of kids to see the dogs is getting pretty long."

Lindsay felt herself blush. She hadn't planned on

staying and talking to Aiden so long but conversing with him was always so easy.

Embarrassed about keeping him from his job, Lindsay excused herself. "It was nice seeing you again. I'll let you get back to work."

Turning on her heel, Lindsay headed over to Alex's side.

ELEVEN

"Why did you do that earlier?" Aiden asked once there was a break from kids wanting to see the dogs.

"What are you talking about?" Zack questioned back in confusion.

"Why did you cut me off when I was talking with Lindsay earlier?"

"Did you see her ring? I did you a favor; you were barking up the wrong tree," Zach stated. "I mean, it's not a deal breaker for me, but you've made it clear it is for you."

Zack was right. Even though Alex wasn't her kid, it didn't mean she wasn't married. He felt foolish for even entertaining the idea of asking her out considering her likely married status.

Not wanting to think about it anymore, Aiden said, as he put Cooper back in his kennel, "I need to go use the bathroom. Can you keep an eye on Cooper for me?"

"Sure, man, no problem."

Aiden left and headed towards the school office. He was pretty sure they would have a restroom he could use.

About half way to the front of the school, Aiden saw Lindsay and Alex playing a dart game at one of the booths. He debated about whether or not to say anything. Before he could make a decision, Lindsay turned around and saw him.

He couldn't help but notice Lindsay looked tempting in her jeans and black sweater. With her blond hair pulled back in a ponytail, it showed off her long neck and gorgeous face.

A hesitant smile developed as she said, "Alex is going to make a great cop when he grows up. He just hit three bullseyes in a row."

Aiden looked past Lindsay to where Alex was standing in front of the dart targets. Sure enough, all three darts were sticking in the center of the target.

"Good job, Alex," Aiden praised.

"Thanks, Officer Aiden," Alex said before turning back to play another round.

Glancing around, Aiden asked with curiosity, "Why didn't your husband come with you tonight?"

Lindsay's brows crinkled together in perplexity. "I'm not married. Whatever gave you that idea?"

He gestured to her hand. "You're wearing a gold band on your left ring finger."

Glancing down at it, she said, "My father gave it to me in junior high. I've worn it ever since."

A sense of relief flooded Aiden as he realized his attraction to Lindsay was no longer inappropriate. "In that case, I was wondering if you would want to go out with me sometime? Maybe this Friday night?"

With a warm grin, she replied, "Yes, I'd love to."

"Can I get your number, so I can text you the details?"

"Sure," Lindsay said telling him her number which he promptly saved in his phone.

As he watched Lindsay leave to find Alex, a sense of elation filled him. For the rest of the night, Aiden couldn't keep his mind from thinking about Lindsay and the prospect of getting to know her better.

TWELVE

A wave of peace passed over Lindsay as she entered Clear Mountain Assembly. Like every Sunday morning, she attended the early-morning church service with her best friend, Erica.

The burdens of the week vanished—if only for a short time—as the welcomed tranquility of the church helped calm the chaos caused by Lindsay's chosen profession.

"Good morning, Lindsay, Erica," Stacy Wingate, the elderly church secretary, greeted them as they entered the double doors to the sanctuary.

Lindsay smiled as she took the bulletin from the other woman's hand. "Good morning, Stacy."

"Hi, Stacy," Erica stated in a chipper mood.

"You both working today during second service?"

Both women nodded.

"I'm going to be in the nursery," Lindsay explained.

Even though she worked with kids all week long, she didn't often get to spend time with the children in a happy environment for any length of time. Knowing she might never have a baby of her own, volunteering in the nursery helped keep her biological clock from going crazy.

"And I'm helping out with the junior high students," Erica stated.

Erica was a bit of a firecracker. Kids were naturally attracted to her ball of energy personality, which made her a perfect fit to work with the pubescent teens.

"You guys are always so dependable; helping out wherever Pastor Steve needs you," Stacy praised. Glancing behind her, Stacy added, "You better go get some seats. Looks like worship is about to start."

The friends made their way down the aisle and deposited themselves about four rows from the front of the moderate sized room.

Moments later, the musicians started to play one of Lindsay's favorite contemporary worship songs. The upbeat music pumped out through the speakers into the sanctuary causing the congregation to clap to the beat and their singing to fill the room.

After the worship ended, everyone took their seats as Pastor Steve moved to the stage. He was dressed in a pair of jeans and a button-up.

Lindsay had grown up going to a more conservative church. When she first started attending Clear Mountain Assembly, it had taken her a few visits to get used to the casual style.

"Good morning, Clear Mountain Assembly. I'm so glad you guys made it today. We're starting a new series called, 'God's Handiwork.'" Pastor Steve looked around the room before continuing. "Some of you might be new to Christianity, and that's okay. We want to help you find the answers you are looking for. Why are you the way you are? Did God design you that way for a reason? And if so, what is it? Others of you might have grown up in church, but never really knew what your purpose was. How do I find my purpose? How do I fulfill it?"

A meme popped up behind the pastor of a baby crying with the caption, "Please don't judge God's handiwork. He isn't finished with me yet."

Laughter rang out across the room and Pastor Steve waited several moments. "You're probably wondering what's keeping us from finding the answers to these questions? The biggest obstacle is accepting that we're all a permanent work-in-progress. Your purpose will always be changing and your calling will grow with you. God's handiwork is a kaleidoscope, and we're all important changing colors that make it work. With one small turn, new beauty is created. All the glass shards work together to create an ever-changing masterpiece. Once you accept this important truth, you can move forward in resolute knowledge."

Lindsay loved the idea of being a changing color in a bigger picture. There was comfort knowing she didn't need to be perfect. As a constant work-in-progress, she needed God to keep molding her.

Pastor Steve concluded his sermon with a prayer before a final worship song played for dismissal.

Erica and Lindsay made their way to the hallway off the lobby where the children and youth ministry was held.

"The message was powerful," Erica said with enthusiasm.

"Agreed. Pastor Steve did a great job."

The friends came to a stop in front of the nursery. "I'll meet you in the lobby after service," Lindsay stated.

"Sure thing," Erica confirmed with a smile before turning on her heel and heading towards the youth room.

Lindsay opened the door to the nursery and went inside. The elderly Maria Lopez was holding one of the Wheaton twins in a chair. "Good morning, Lindsay." She pointed to the other twin. "You should probably grab Bryce before he starts crying."

With a nod, Lindsay picked up the nine-month-old baby and sat in one of the nearby rocking chairs. She brushed his blond curls from his forehead and smiled at him. The little boy returned the grin, revealing one tiny tooth poking up from his lower gums.

Though she had held many children throughout her time as a social worker, often the situation was tense, and the child was crying. It felt good to hold a baby in a relaxed environment without trepidation.

"How was your week?" Maria asked.

"Difficult. I'm still looking for a home for one of my kids. He's been in a temporary shelter group home for two weeks now. He's not adjusting well, and I suspect he is being bullied."

"I'm sorry to hear that." A compassionate look formed on Maria's face. "I will pray for him."

"Thank you."

"Are you dating anyone right now? I haven't seen you with any new fella around here," Maria probed.

"I do have a date on Friday night."

Excitement filled Maria's voice as she spoke. "You

have to tell me all about him. How did you meet? Is he handsome? I hope it wasn't one of those online things," Maria stated with distaste. "I just don't get how all that works."

Shaking her head, Lindsay explained, "No, I bumped into him downtown a couple of weeks ago and then again at Happy's a few days later. One of my kids ran up to him because he was in uniform; he's a K-9 officer. He's good-looking and friendly."

Maria nodded. "Where does he go to church?"

Lindsay's stomach clenched. She didn't know if Aiden even went to church, let alone if he was a Christian. How could she have overlooked something so important? As Aiden's handsome dimpled cheeks and sultry smile flashed through her mind, she realized she had been focused on other things. She made a note to herself she would have to ask him about his religious background on their date.

Avoiding answering, Lindsay asked, "How was your week?"

"Oh, you know, same old, same old. I took care of the grandkids for my daughter while she was at work."

"Don't dismiss what you do," Lindsay stated. "You're amazing for taking care of your family."

Maria met Lindsay's eyes. "I appreciate your kind words. I always wondered if I should have gotten a job after Frank died, but Lucinda needed my help after her divorce, so I moved in with her to help."

"God sees your sacrifice and is grateful," Lindsay promised. "As I'm sure your daughter is too."

"She tells me so all the time," Maria smiled. "Now, if I could just get her to come to church with me, I would be a happy old woman."

"Then we shall pray for it," Lindsay offered.

The two of them spent the rest of the time in the nursery praying while taking care of the three babies in their care.

THIRTEEN

"Come on," Aiden yelled at the television screen, "that's a bad call, ref." Throwing his hands up in the air, Aiden reached out and took a swig of his beer.

Even though it was Sunday, he should probably be at the gym rather than at home watching the game, but like any true born and raised Coloradoan, Aiden was a die-hard Denver Bronco's fan. It made the potential defeat by the Dallas Cowboys especially painful to watch.

Though raised in a church-going family, after his parents' sudden death while he was in college, Aiden stopped attending church regularly. On occasion—mostly during the major Christian holidays—Aiden would make the effort to go to his old church out of nostalgia. On a regular basis, however, Aiden would much rather sleep in and watch sports instead of going to the stifling church from his childhood.

Standing up, Aiden stretched before heading towards the kitchen to grab another beer and a fresh slice of pizza.

Cooper jumped up from his spot on the couch and followed Aiden into the other room.

"What? Are you wanting a treat, boy?" Aiden asked with a grin.

Reaching on top of the fridge, Aiden grabbed a canister. Unscrewing the top, he pulled out a dog biscuit and extended it to Cooper, who immediately gobbled it up in two bites.

"That was fast."

Aiden looked down at Cooper and noticed the pleading look in his partner's eyes. Giving in, he sighed and pulled out another treat.

"Here you go, boy." Aiden offered the second dog biscuit to Cooper. "This is the last one though. We got to keep you in shape now, don't we?"

Glancing at the half-eaten pizza on the counter, Aiden decided not to take another piece. "Considering I need to do the same, I should probably refrain from having anymore myself."

After closing the lid to the pizza, Aiden opened the fridge and grabbed a bottle of water instead of another beer from inside. Keeping physically fit was an important part of working search and rescue. Though the call-outs were sporadic at best, the adrenaline he got from those assignments surpassed any other type of calls. He didn't want to miss out on them because he let himself go physically.

"Let's go finish the game, boy," Aiden said as he walked back in the living room.

Before he could sit back down, a knock sounded at the door. He made his way over and opened it. Zach stood on the other side.

"Hey, man, I figured since it's Sunday, you'd be at home with the game on. Can I come in?" Zach asked with Harley next to him.

With a nonchalant shrug, Aiden moved out of the way to let Zach and Harley enter. "There's pizza on the counter and beer in the fridge."

Harley jumped up onto the couch next to Cooper while Zach made his way into the kitchen. He helped himself to the food before taking a seat in the recliner next to the couch.

"Sorry I showed up so late," Zach said as he took a bite of pizza. "I finally got last night's date to leave."

Shaking his head, Aiden asked, "Don't you ever get tired of your revolving door of badge bunnies?"

Zack snorted. "Never. I like my bachelor lifestyle." Taking another bite of pizza, he asked, "How about you? Have you closed the deal with that hot blond from Happy's and the carnival?"

An irritated scowl formed on Aiden's face. "I haven't even taken her out on a date yet. That's happening on Friday."

"Man, why waste time dating her? Just call her up and hit that."

"No way. That's not my style."

"Have you ever even gone out on a real date? I mean, all you have to do is go to a cop bar and the badge bunnies just flock to you."

Aiden shrugged. "I've never needed to make much of an effort. How hard can it be?"

"Ah, man, you've got your work cut out for you. You better plan something nice for a girl like that. I bet she's going to be high maintenance."

"I think you're wrong. Lindsay seems down-to-earth."

"Suit yourself." Zach rolled his eyes. "But don't say I didn't warn you."

Changing the subject, Aiden said, "I'm glad you brought Harley to spend some time with Cooper. I think he misses her on our days off."

"You think so?" Zach asked, looking over at the two dogs who were curled up together on the couch.

"I guess it makes sense." Looking at the TV, Zach inquired, "How are the Broncos doing?"

"They're down by five but if they can make a touchdown, they can still win this."

Just then, the game came back on from break and the men settled into their seats to watch the last quarter.

FOURTEEN

Excited anticipation was pulsating through Lindsay's body. In a few minutes, Aiden O'Connell was going to pick her up for their first date. She wondered what he'd planned? Dinner at one of the hip and modern restaurants downtown? Or maybe ice skating at the local rink?

She looked over at the clock on her nightstand, 6:55 PM. He should be arriving any minute and she assumed, due to his job, he was the punctual type.

Taking a final look in the mirror in her bathroom, she adjusted her blue dress and smoothed out her blond hair. She exited her room and found Erica sitting in the living room watching TV.

Erica glanced up from the couch and smiled. "You

look great, Lindsay. Aiden isn't gonna know what hit him when you answer the door."

Lindsay's heart warmed from the compliment. "Thanks, Erica. Sorry your date cancelled on you tonight."

With a small shrug, Erica said, "What are you going to do? It's one of the pitfalls of online dating. At least he had the decency to cancel before I showed up at the restaurant. No shows are the worst."

Lindsay nodded. It was another reason she disliked online dating, but it seemed to keep Erica happy.

The doorbell rang. Lindsay's attention was drawn to it. She made her way over to the front door of their apartment.

On the other side stood Aiden dressed in a leather jacket, jeans, and a white t-shirt with his hands shoved in his pockets. Though he looked handsome as always, his appearance was rather casual for a first date.

"You look nice," Aiden said with attractive smile. "You ready to go?"

"Sure," she said leaning over and grabbing her purse and jacket from the entry table.

"Have a good time," Erica shouted from the couch.

Glancing past her, he asked, "Who's that?"

"My roommate and friend Erica," Lindsay answered as she stepped out of the apartment and pulled the door shut behind her.

"You're going to lock that, right?" Aiden asked.

Her eyebrows came together in confusion. "Why? Erica's home."

"Because you don't want to make it easy for a burglary to happen. You'd be surprised how many are preventable simply by locking a door. Criminals look for opportunities and unlocked doors are a big one."

"Always on duty, aren't you, Officer O'Connell," she stated with a laugh. Turning around, she pulled her key out of her purse and locked the door.

At the end of the walkway, Aiden had a convertible red Mustang waiting for them. Lindsay waited to see if Aiden would open her door, but he made no gesture to do so. Instead, he walked around to the driver's side door and slid into the leather seat.

Shocked by his lack of proper dating etiquette, Lindsay waffled on whether to get in the sports car with Aiden. Was he honestly unaware how ungentlemanly it was to not open the car door for her?

From inside the vehicle, he gestured for her. Against her better judgment, Lindsay opened the car door and joined Aiden.

"Where are you taking me?"

"It's a surprise. I think you'll like it."

She noticed he glanced over at her a few times before he asked, "So what's with the ring? I know you said your father gave it to you, but why do you wear it on your ring finger?"

Lindsay looked down at her left hand and rubbed her other thumb along it. "It's my promise ring. My dad gave it to me on my thirteenth birthday."

"I think I remember hearing about that at church. It's a promise to God to wait until marriage to be intimate, right?"

Lindsay stiffened under the direct question. The ring never had to be explained before. She hadn't dated in high school as she cared more about working with horses on her dad's ranch than boys. Then while she was in college, she had met Rick in church, so the ring and the commitment behind it was never an issue.

She decided it was best to be direct. If Aiden was hoping to get her into bed, it was best she find out now before this date went any further. "Yes, that's right. Is that a problem for you?"

He shook his head. "No, I think it's admirable that you made that choice. I can't say I've done the same, but I respect it."

"Thank you. You mentioned you knew what the ring was from going to church? I go to Clear Mountain Assembly, but I've never seen you there. Do you go to another church in town?"

"I *used* to go. My parents took me when I was a kid, but once I was in college, I stopped."

Lindsay wondered why he quit going. She knew it wasn't uncommon for Christians to have their faith questioned when they were in college. Lindsay herself had it happen, but she dove stronger into her faith to counteract it. What kept Aiden from doing the same?

"Why did you stop going?"

She noticed his hands tighten on the steering wheel and he paused several seconds before answering. "My parents died in an automobile accident while I was in college. I didn't see the point in going after that."

"I'm so sorry, Aiden. How awful. Do you have other family?"

"I have an older brother, but he went to college back east. He stayed out there after he graduated. We talk every once-in-awhile on the phone, but he's busy with his job and family." He looked over at her and smiled. "How about you? You mentioned your father but not your mother."

Lindsay didn't know they would get into such personal matters on a first date. Of course, it was her own doing since she started asking him about his family first. She supposed she should reciprocate. "My mom died from cancer when I was ten. My dad never remarried."

"Do you see him often?"

She shook her head. "He's not the best company. He didn't handle my mother's death well, so when I got a full scholarship to the University of Colorado, I moved out and didn't look back."

"Do you have any siblings?"

Lindsay shook her head. "I'm an only child; my mother couldn't have any more kids after me." She didn't offer any more information on the subject, not wanting to explain she had the same difficulties her mother had which prevented successful pregnancies.

"We're here," Aiden said.

Looking out the window of the car, she saw that they were parked in front of "The Lucky Penny" bar.

"I brought you back to the place where we met," Aiden stated with a prideful grin.

Aversion creeped into Lindsay's mind. She tried to swallow the lump of disgust that formed in her throat.

Why had he brought her here? Bars were the worst place to bring someone on a first date. The few times she went to one in college with friends, the noise was overpowering and the patrons were often obnoxious.

"Let's get inside before it starts raining again," Aiden suggested.

With reservation, Lindsay opened the car door and climbed out. If the bar was anything like the ones she had been in before, this was going to be a short date.

FIFTEEN

As Aiden walked into the bar with Lindsay by his side, the familiarity of the place washed over him. For only being a little after seven at night, the bar was buzzing with regulars.

Bon Jovi's "Wanted Dead or Alive" was playing on the juke box in the corner. Next to it was a set of pool tables and a dart board on the wall.

Several of the off-duty cops glanced over at them and gave a nod and a wave to Aiden who returned the gesture. Not wanting to get bogged down in a conversation with any of them, Aiden avoided going over to the bar-top. Instead, he turned to Lindsay and asked, "You up for a game of pool?"

Her eyes darted around the room and after a moment's pause, she answered with a hesitant voice, "I suppose."

They made their way over to the empty table. Each of them grabbed a pool stick, then Aiden took the balls and a triangle from underneath. As he set the game up for the first shot, he asked, "Do you play pool much?"

"Not really," Lindsay said in a terse voice. "I generally try to avoid places like this."

Before he could pose a follow-up question, a woman's sultry voice from the side said, "Why if it isn't Officer Aiden O'Connell as I live and breathe."

Great, Chantel. Aiden stiffened under the unwelcome company. Maybe bringing Lindsay here wasn't the greatest idea. Originally, he thought it would be fun to bring her back to where they met, but he didn't think about the fact he might have to fend off badge bunnies all night.

Chantel came into focus as her hand snaked out to drape over his arm. "Haven't seen you in here much these days."

"I've been busy, Chantel."

"What's a girl got to do to get you to pay her a little attention?" she asked in a flirtatious voice as she leaned in even closer, making sure her ample chest was in his line of sight.

Uncomfortable with Chantel's persistence, especially in front of Lindsay, his eyes flickered over to his date. Lindsay didn't look pleased with the interaction between Aiden and the other woman. If he had any chance of redeeming this night, he needed to get rid of Chantel A-SAP.

"Chantel, I want to introduce you to my date, Lindsay."

"Date?" she squeaked out in disbelief as her hand jerked off of his arm. "My, my, I never thought I would see the day." With a heavy sigh, she said, "I guess I need to go find someone else to occupy my time." Her eyes moved over to Lindsay for a moment before she added with a sly smile. "Sorry he brought you here, honey. Not the best place for a date, but then, most of these cops stick to a pretty basic routine."

After Chantel sauntered off, Aiden gave Lindsay a sheepish grin. "Sorry about that."

One of her eyebrows arched as she said, "Are we going to have to deal with that all night?"

"I hope not," he stated as he bent down and took the break shot.

The balls went spinning across the table, several of them making a deposit into different pockets.

"I can see you spend a lot of time doing this," Lindsay observed.

"I used to," Aiden hesitated, not wanting to talk about Veronica or his tailspin of skirt-chasing after, "but not so much the past few months. Lately, I only come here when Zach drags me out."

"Did I hear my name?"

Great, Zach. Could this night get any worse? With a heavy sigh, Aiden turned to his partner and asked, "What are you doing here?"

"I always come here on Friday nights. You know that."

That's right. Aiden did know that. What had he been thinking coming here? This confirmed his earlier thoughts that it was a mistake to bring Lindsay to The Lucky Penny.

"I see you got the blond to go out with you." Looking Lindsay up and down, he added in a sleazy tone, "Nice."

She must have picked up on the way he stared at her because an embarrassed look crossed Lindsay's face before her eyes dropped to the floor.

"Zach, why don't you head over to the bar and talk up Chantel?" Adding in a warning tone, Aiden said, "We're good here."

Zach lifted up his hands in a sign of surrender. "Whoa, man, didn't mean to upset you." Turning around, he headed towards the bar.

"Are you okay?" Aiden asked.

"Aiden, I think it's best if we just call it a night," Lindsay stated. She glanced around, and added, "You can stay here, and I can get an Uber."

Setting down his pool stick; Aiden shook his head. "No need for that. I'll take you home."

As they made their way out of the bar, Aiden noticed Lindsay's dejected face. He felt like a complete jerk; he should have put more effort into planning the date. Dating had never been hard for him. When he was young, the girls flocked to him because of the combination of his boy-next-door good looks and jock status. Then when he became a cop, the badge erased any remaining obstacles. This was the first time a woman didn't fall for his usual dating style which left him off-kilter.

The ride home was quiet. Aiden wanted to fix his mistake, but he wasn't sure how to do it. As soon as he parked the car, Lindsay opened the door and climbed out. He rushed around to join her, but she didn't seem to be waiting for him.

"I wanted to apologize for what happened tonight."

Without looking at him, Lindsay raised her hand towards him. "No need, Aiden. I learned a valuable lesson tonight; I'm not interested in dating someone who would take me to a bar on a date. I should've said something when we first got there, but I didn't which is my fault."

"Can I have a do-over?" Aiden implored.

"What good would it do? We're obviously not a good fit; we don't want the same things in life. Let's just call it quits before it gets worse."

Aiden wanted to object, but he could see her mind was made up. Giving in, Aiden nodded. "If that's what you think's best."

"I do."

Crestfallen, Aiden turned around and headed back down the walkway. He got in his car but when he went to put the car in drive, he froze. Glancing up at Lindsay's door, he noticed she was already inside.

What was wrong with him? He really liked Lindsay and he just acted like a buffoon. The type of women he usually dated would be fine going to The Lucky Penny, but Lindsay was different. As soon as he knew about her religious background, he should have changed his plans. Correction: his lack of plans. She deserved better than how he treated her tonight.

It had been a long time since he prayed. If he really thought about it, he hadn't since he went away to college. But the urge to do so surfaced and the words took form with little effort. "God, I need your help . . . I messed up tonight. I don't know what it is, but there is something about Lindsay that makes me want to find a way to convince her to give me a second chance. Show me what I need to do."

Aiden opened his eyes and felt a peace take root in his heart. An idea took form in his mind. As he drove off, Aiden knew what he had to do.

SIXTEEN

Two boys came whizzing by as Lindsay stepped into the entry of the shelter group home. Though Saturday was her day off, she needed something to occupy her mind. She woke up still disappointed from the night before. Her date with Aiden was painful to say the least. She hadn't wanted to stay around the apartment playing twenty questions about what went wrong with Erica.

"Good morning, Miss Wright," Linda Stanton greeted as she dodged two more children who ran past them.

Linda was an older brunette woman with a small frame and friendly disposition. For the past three months, she had been in charge of the shelter group home, but it had become increasingly difficult to manage. Due to the lack of qualified foster families, the home was filled beyond what was normal.

"What brings you by today?" Linda asked.

Lindsay glanced around the room before answering. Alex was usually one of the first kids to run down the stairs and greet her. Where was he?

A pensive look formed on Linda's face. "Did Alex call you? I told him not to bother you and I would take care of it."

Lindsay's eyes snapped to Linda. "No, I was bringing by his sweater. He forgot it when he was in my care the other day. What are you talking about?"

"These things happen, Miss Wright. I do my best to keep the boys from going at each other, but sometimes it's unavoidable."

Pushing past the other woman, Lindsay made her way farther into the house. "Where's Alex? Did something happen to him?"

"He's resting in the living room. I asked him what happened when I found him at the bottom of the stairs, but he won't tell me."

Lindsay marched into the other room where Alex was sitting on one of the couches watching TV.

Lindsay came over and sat next to him on the couch. "Hey there, Alex."

The boy's eyes momentarily flickered to Lindsay. The mixture of fear, hurt and worry she saw in his gaze made her heart break. As quickly as it appeared, Alex masked it and looked away.

"Do you want to tell me what happened?"

"It doesn't matter."

"Of course it matters," Lindsay countered. "Just tell me what happened, and I can help."

"I slipped."

"You don't have to do that Alex," Lindsay said as she reached out and placed her hand on his arm. "You don't have to cover for whoever pushed you."

"It's what happened, so you might as well leave," Alex stated adamantly as he pulled away. "There's no point in sticking around here."

Lindsay didn't want to leave, but she could see she wasn't getting anywhere with Alex at the moment. She could try back later in the week and hope he had a change of heart.

Standing up, Lindsay said, "You can call me anytime, Alex." She waited several seconds, but when there was no response, she turned to exit the room.

Linda was standing in the doorframe with her arms crossed. As Lindsay approached her, she said, "I told you he won't tell the truth about what happened."

Lindsay wanted to yell at Linda. It was her job to protect Alex, but she knew it wouldn't do any good.

Instead she offered some advice. "I just want to make sure you're aware of the importance of supervising Alex's interactions with the older boys and keeping them separated. I think it's in everyone's best interest."

"I'm doing the best I can, Miss Wright. There really should be two caregivers for this many boys, but they don't have anyone to assign to work with me here."

Lindsay nodded. "I know you're doing all you can under the circumstances. I'll be back later in the week to check on Alex."

Once inside her car, Lindsay leaned back against the headrest in frustration. She wanted to get Alex into a new foster home, but every time she checked the database for new potentials, she came up empty handed.

Her heart ached from the bad week she was having. She couldn't keep Alex from being bullied which made her feel useless. Coupled with the terrible date with Aiden, she couldn't keep the tears from falling.

"Dear Lord, I need your strength to deal with all of this. Help me do what is right for Alex and to get him out of this place before something worse happens. I also ask that you help me get over my date with Aiden last night. I shouldn't care this much about what happened, yet I can't seem to shake this sullenness in my heart. In Jesus' name, I pray, Amen."

Lindsay turned the key in the ignition and headed home.

SEVENTEEN

Zach and Aiden's Saturday afternoon of playing video games was interrupted by the call-out for a mudslide involving two vehicles with multiple potential victims.

Aiden tried to concentrate on preparing himself for the situation, but his mind kept drifting back to his conversation with Zach earlier in the day.

"You're going to do what?" Zach's eyes grew wide with shock.

"I'm going to church tomorrow."

"Since when is that a priority for you?"

"Since I met Lindsay. She's worth it. Besides, I used to go to church all the time growing up."

"And there must be a reason you stopped."

Aiden stiffened under the judgment, but realized it was

true. "My parents were killed in a car accident while I was in college. I stopped going because I blamed God."

Zach averted his eyes. "I'm sorry, man. I didn't know."

"I don't talk about it much."

"I still don't understand why you got to go to church," Zach scoffed.

"I'm starting to see that the reason I'm attracted to Lindsay is because of her faith. I've never felt this way about a woman and I want to do whatever it takes to get her to give me a second chance."

"K-9 2, this is dispatch, how far out are you from the mudslide location?" Deanna's voice over the radio jarred Aiden out of his thoughts. "Reporting party is stating that a secondary slide has occurred and buried another car under the debris."

Aiden picked up the receiver from the car's radio. "Copy that, Dispatch, this is K-9 2. We are less than five minutes from the location. Will radio with update once we arrive on scene and assess the situation."

Zach was behind the wheel, pushing the SUV as hard as he could with lights and sirens broadcasting their approach. Though windy and lined with massive trees on both sides, Zach expertly handled the curvy road until he brought the vehicle to a halt at the reported location.

Both officers jumped out of the SUV and swiftly moved around to the back to get their K-9 partners.

With Cooper and Harley on leash, they walked over to where an elderly couple were standing at the shoulder of the road.

"Can one of you tell us what you witnessed?" Zach inquired.

"My name is Walter Stein, and this is my wife, Stella. We didn't actually see the first car get swept away, but we were behind the second vehicle." The older man paused before continuing, "They were trying to get around the debris from the first mudslide, when another section of the mountain gave way."

"We barely avoided getting caught in it ourselves," Stella said with a shaky voice. "It was a mini-van and I saw a child in the back." Turning to Aiden with tears in her eyes, she added, "You have to help them, Officer."

"We'll do everything we can," Aiden promised.

"I would have tried to get down there myself, but I just had a hip replacement," Walter explained. "We only know there were two cars because when we stopped to try to help the second car, we saw the headlights of the other car under the mud."

Aiden looked down the edge of the mountain. He realized Walter was right; it would've proved too difficult for a man of Walter's age and limited mobility, but Aiden was certain they could reach the cars.

"Why don't the both of you get back in your car and wait where it's safe," Zach urged. "I'd tell you to head back to Clear Mountain, but somehow I don't think you will."

Walter and Stella shook their heads. "We want to make sure they're alright, Officer," Walter stated.

"But we'll keep a safe distance and wait in our car like you suggested," Stella added, before the couple turned around and walked to the vehicle.

"Search and Rescue 1, this is K-9 2, what's your ETA?" Aiden asked over the radio.

"K-9 2, this is Search and Rescue 1, the rest of the team is ten minutes out."

"Copy that, Search and Rescue 1," Aiden said. "We're going to start to descend now and see what we can find. Radio us when you get here." Taking a moment's break, Aiden gestured down, and Zach nodded; they had developed a non-verbal shorthand over the past year and both knew what they needed to do. "Dispatch, this is K-9 2. We're on scene and have talked to reporting party. Search and Rescue 1 is on the way. K-9 1 and 2 are going to descend to the trapped cars now to start the search for victims."

"Copy that, K-9 2. Keep us posted on your progress."

Zach and Aiden made their way over to the edge of the road before unhooking Cooper and Harley from their leashes.

"You ready, boy?" Aiden encouraged.

Barking in reply, Cooper kept his eyes on Aiden and waited for the command to search.

Given the cue, Cooper took off, followed by Harley once Zach gave permission. Aiden and Zach brought up the rear of the search party, making sure to carefully move through the debris while scanning for any signs of life.

They came upon the mini-van first. Most of the front end was covered in debris, leaving only the back hatch visible. Aiden leaned forward and brushed the mud from the glass to see inside. There was a woman in the driver's seat along with a baby strapped into a carseat in the middle row; neither of them were moving.

"What can you see?" Zach asked as he pulled his pack from his back.

Turning to Zach, Aiden took off his own pack and started digging inside. "There's two victims; one adult female and one infant." Pulling out a spring-loaded punch tool, he added, "I'm going to break the glass now. Stand back."

"Dispatch, this is K-9 1. We have eyes on two victims inside one of the vehicles. K-9 2 is going to enter the vehicle to assess the occupants." Zach updated over the radio as he stepped out of the way.

Aiden placed the punch against the glass and released the spring. The glass shattered, and he was able to push it out of the way. He reached inside and unlocked the hatch, then pulled it open to gain access.

He climbed inside and crawled to the carseat. Gently, he reached out and touched the baby's arm. Dressed in blue, he assumed it was a boy who looked to be about six-months-old. The baby opened his eyes and smiled with a coo.

Quickly, Aiden undid the restraints and lifted the baby out of the carseat. He made his way back through the vehicle and handed the baby off to Zach.

As Aiden climbed back through the car, he heard Zach's voice over the radio say, "Dispatch, this is K-9 1. We've safely secured one of the victims; a male infant. K-9 2 is re-entering the vehicle to evaluate the driver."

Reaching out, Aiden placed his hand on the woman's shoulder. "Ma'am, can you hear me? My name is Officer O'Connell and I'm with Clear Mountain Search and Rescue."

The woman stirred, and her eyes fluttered open. She turned her head to him as a confused look formed. "What's going on?"

"You've been in an accident," he explained. "Are you feeling pain anywhere?"

She nodded, then grimaced. "My head is pounding and my left arm hurts."

Glancing at her head, he saw blood pouring from her nose. She probably broke it when the airbag deployed; a common injury but not one that needed immediate treatment. Leaning across her, he looked at her arm. A large gash on her upper arm was bleeding. Since she was moving the rest of her body, she didn't seem to have any other visible injuries.

Aiden pulled out a bandana from his back pocket and pushed it against the wound, then grabbed her arm and placed it over the makeshift bandage. "Keep pressure here while I help get you out of your van. You're going to have to crawl out first while I follow behind."

Once they were both out of the car, Aiden helped her sit on the ground a safe distance away. Taking the baby from Zach, Aiden said, "Why don't you and Harley go see if you can locate the other car?"

With a nod, Zach took off with Harley by his side.

"How are you feeling," Aiden asked as he handed her the infant.

She glanced down at the baby and then around the area as a worried look formed. "Where's Kylie?"

"Who?" Aiden asked, confused.

"My daughter. She was in the seat next to her brother."

Aiden's stomach clenched with dread. He hadn't seen anyone else in the car. Where was the little girl?

"I just started letting her put her seatbelt on herself. She constantly unbuckles it. I remember telling her to put it back on right before the mudslide hit the car." Panic started to creep into the woman's voice. "Where is she? Where's my daughter?"

Bending down, he forced himself not to react to the woman's tears or the fear in her eyes. "Ma'am, you need to tell me, is there anything in the car that belonged to her?"

Nodding, the woman pushed out through her crying, "I have a diaper bag in the car. I keep a spare set of clothes in it for Kylie because she still has accidents."

"Stay calm, ma'am. My partner, Cooper here, is trained to find missing persons. We're going to find your daughter."

He left out the fact finding her wasn't the issue. What condition she was in when he did was what concerned Aiden. If the little girl had been ejected during the crash, it was unlikely she survived.

Trying not to focus on the grim probability, Aiden stood up and headed towards the back of the van. He climbed in and found the diaper bag on the floorboard of the front passenger seat. He pulled out the pink shirt with tiny flowers on it.

"Dispatch, this is K-9 2. I was just informed by the driver that there was a third occupant in the car. A female child is missing. Show K-9 2 as initiating search."

Jumping out of the vehicle, he put the shirt to Cooper's nose, allowing him to breathe in the scent. After making sure he got a good imprint, Aiden gestured for Cooper to hunt.

Before they got far, the rest of the Clear Mountain Search and Rescue arrived. As they approached, the head of the unit, Sergeant Burton, stated, "O'Connell, we heard over the radio what is going on. I'm going to assign Hendrick and Blaze to help you search for the missing girl, while Tackett and myself head over to help Zach with the other vehicle."

"Sounds good, Sarge." Aiden glanced around and lowered his voice. "What if this turns out to be recovery rather than rescue, given the circumstances?"

"We'll deal with that if it comes to it, but my guess is no matter what her condition, she won't be far from the initial mudslide area."

The other two men came up to Aiden and waited for his instructions. "Alright, Hendricks and Blaze, take the south side while Cooper and myself take the north side."

The men split up and worked their way through the area, following Cooper's lead.

A few minutes later, Cooper started barking and circling an area. Aiden sprinted to the spot where he found a still, small form covered in debris, sticking out of the mud.

His heart plummeted to his stomach. Instantly, he knew it was the little girl. Dropping to his knees beside her, he reached out and pulled her from the refuse.

Though she had a few scratches, she otherwise seemed intact. He placed his fingertips on her wrist. *No pulse*. He put his face to her mouth. *No breathing. She was still warm which meant her vital signs hadn't been compromised for long.* Immediately, he began chest compressions, followed by breaths. He repeated the pattern two more times before checking for results. *Nothing*. He started again.

On the second round, Blaze arrived next to him and took over breathing. The two continued to work on the little girl, and just when Aiden had given up hope, the little girl sputtered and coughed. He rolled her to the side and started to gently pat her back, saying, "It's alright, sweetie. That's it; get it out, get it out."

Once she was stable, Aiden gathered her up in his arms and carried her over to her waiting mother. As he handed the girl to the bawling woman, through the sobs, she sputtered out, "Thank you, thank you, Officer. You saved my baby."

As Aiden requested an ambulance to take the family to the hospital, a sense of satisfaction took hold in his heart. Sometimes he thought he did the job for the adrenaline, but as he looked down at the mother and child he just reunited, Aiden knew he did it for them.

EIGHTEEN

Lindsay listened intently to Pastor Steve's second part of his series, "God's Handiwork." She could feel God doing a work in her as she listened to the truth and let it ruminate in her heart.

"You were created in God's image. He doesn't make mistakes. To put yourself down for the way He made you is to insult God's handiwork. Ephesians 2:10 says, 'We are God's handiwork, created in Christ Jesus to do good works.' So, don't think of your limitations as a handicap, but rather as an asset God will use to change the world."

How many times had Lindsay beat herself up over Rick leaving her because of her inability to have children? She had spent the last couple of years feeling flawed and broken, as if her endometriosis somehow made her inferior to other women who had functioning reproductive systems. Yet, as she sat and listened to the pastor, she realized that God wouldn't use her despite her disease, but He would use her *because* of her disease to help others. The right man would see that and want to adopt with her, and they could help a child feel loved who otherwise would never have that.

"I didn't think this week's message could be better than last week's, but it seems that Pastor Steve outdid himself," Erica stated as they made their way to the back of the church.

"I know. It's exactly what I needed to hear."

Just as they reached the double doors leading out of the sanctuary, Aiden came into view, stepping out from one of the back rows of chairs.

Lindsay's eyes grew round with surprise. "What are you doing here?"

Glancing around the room, he asked, "Can we talk somewhere more private?"

"I guess," Lindsay agreed. Then turning to Erica, she said, "I'll catch up with you later."

Aiden, with Lindsay following, moved over to a back corner of the sanctuary.

"The sermon was good. I like your pastor and the worship is different than what we had at the church I used to go to. I like it."

"I'm glad to hear it. Is that why you came here? To check out my church? I mean, don't get me wrong, I'm glad you decided to come to church, but you could have gone anywhere else and it would have been less awkward."

Aiden shook his head. "No, I also came because I want to apologize," Aiden began. "I made a mistake the other night when I took you to The Lucky Penny. I should've put more effort into the evening. You deserve better than that."

"Is that what you do on a typical weekend?"

Moving towards her, he reached out and grabbed her hands. "It is . . . I mean it used to be, but not anymore. I want to do more than that and be with someone who wants more than that." With sincerity in his eyes, he pleaded, "Are you willing to give me a second chance? I promise I won't disappoint you again."

Something inside Lindsay made her want to believe Aiden. He seemed genuine and he had shown up at church after all. She found herself agreeing to his request. "Fine, I will give you one more chance; but Aiden, this is it. You won't get a third chance."

"You won't regret it," Aiden stated with a charming grin. "Thanks for taking another chance on me."

NINETEEN

As Lindsay got ready for her do-over date with Aiden, she hoped the second chance she was giving him wouldn't be wasted.

At least she'd had a positive work week which had gone smoother than the past couple. There was a potential new family for Alex. Once the foster parents passed the final stages and were approved, Lindsay could give Alex the good news.

Lindsay put on a dab of vanilla perfume before grabbing her black shawl to go over her fuchsia dress. She made her way downstairs and came into the living room. Erica was sitting in her usual spot on the couch, watching TV.

"I can't believe you're giving that guy another chance. What kind of idiot takes a classy woman to a bar on a first date? I mean, he's hot and all, but he doesn't seem to have a lot going on between the ears."

Lindsay surprised herself by clamoring to Aiden's defense. "No argument, he made a mistake in where he took me, but he was rather articulate in the conversation we did have."

"I hope you don't regret your decision," Erica warned.

A moment later, the doorbell rang, prompting Lindsay to make her way over to the front of the apartment. On the other side of the door was Aiden wearing a pair of black slacks and a blue button-up shirt. In his hands was a bouquet of red roses which he offered to her. "Good evening, Lindsay. These are for you."

Taking the flowers from him, she let her face drift down to them and inhaled the sweet scent. "Thank you. Give me a moment while I hand these off to Erica."

Turning around, she walked over to the couch and gave the flowers to her roommate. "Do you mind putting these in water for me?"

Erica's eyebrows arched in a pleased expression. "Sure." Lowering her voice, she added, "Score one for Officer O'Connell."

Lindsay nodded with a smile. "I know, right?"

"You ready to go?" Aiden asked when she returned to the door.

With a nod, she let Aiden take her arm and guide her over to the car. He opened the passenger door for her and helped her inside. It was a welcome change from their first date.

Once he joined her inside the Mustang, Aiden smiled over at her. "You look really pretty in that dress."

"Thank you," Lindsay said. "You look nice as well. I like seeing you dressed up like that."

He gave her a playful smirk. "I don't do it often since I prefer wearing jeans and a t-shirt on my days off, but you're worth it."

Taking the compliment, Lindsay replied, "Well, I appreciate the effort."

As Aiden drove, Lindsay noticed the familiar buildings of downtown start to dot the streets. She stiffened as they turned down Third Street where The Lucky Penny was located. He wouldn't be audacious enough to try to take her there again, would he?

Just as she started to form the question, they passed the bar and continued on down the road. Lindsay relaxed in the leather seat.

Aiden made a left turn onto "H" Street and after two blocks, pulled into a parking spot in front of Domenico's Italian Restaurant.

"I love this place," Lindsay said with a smile. "Italian food is my favorite."

"Glad to hear it," Aiden said as he put the car into park and turned the engine off. He jumped out of the driver's seat and made his way around to her. Opening her door, he helped her out, then placed her hand in the crook of his arm.

When they entered the restaurant, the owner, Domenico De Luca, rushed up to their sides with a huge grin on his face.

"Good evening, Officer O'Connell. I have your table right this way."

One of Lindsay's eyebrows arched up in surprise at the owner's reaction. She had been coming here with her parents since she was a child, but never received such a reaction from Mr. De Luca.

The table was set gorgeously, with glistening white china and gleaming silverware standing out nicely against the black tablecloth. In the center of the table was another vase of roses and tall candelabras on either side. Lindsay glanced around the room and noticed that none of the other tables had such elaborate decor.

Once they were seated, Mr. De Luca handed them each a menu and returned momentarily with a bottle of wine. He poured them each a glass and gave them a wink. "It's on the house," he informed them before turning around and scurrying off towards the kitchen.

"Do you drink?" Aiden inquired.

"I don't normally consume alcohol, but since Mr. De Luca gave the wine as a gift, I'll have a glass." Lifting the drink to her mouth, she took a sip. "I'm curious, you have to tell me why Mr. De Luca is treating you like you're a celebrity."

"I got a call-out for a disturbing the peace complaint regarding a customer who was causing a scene over a mistake on a to-go order. I diffused the situation, calming down the customer while keeping the fight from escalating. Mr. De Luca was so grateful with how I handled the scenario, he told me to come back any time and he would make my dinner extra special." A sheepish grin formed on Aiden's mouth as he added, "I didn't have a reason to take him up on his offer until now."

Lindsay was pleased to hear that Aiden cared about the citizens he helped while he was working, and that in return, they appreciated his service. It was a testament to his character to have a man like Mr. De Luca approve of him. "I can tell you must have made quite an impression for him to go to all this trouble."

A few moments later, the restaurant owner placed

a bruschetta platter in front of them. "Enjoy," he said with another wink and then disappeared again.

Before they began, Lindsay reached out and took Aiden's hand in her own. "Can we pray before we start eating?"

With a nod, he gripped her hand, and then bowed his head.

"Dear Lord, thank you for this day," Lindsay began. "I pray you bless our time together as well as this food to our bodies. In Jesus' name, I pray, Amen."

Lindsay opened her eyes and looked across the table at Aiden. He didn't seem at all uncomfortable with her request, but rather at peace with it. He not only seemed to accept her faith but looked as if he was starting to find a measure of his own again.

TWENTY

Aiden glanced down at Lindsay's hand in his own. A warm sensation shot up his arm. She wasn't pulling away. That was a good sign, wasn't it?

As Lindsay took another sip of the wine, he let himself take in her good looks. She really was a breathtakingly beautiful woman with her long blond hair and gorgeous green eyes. It would be easy to get lost in their mesmerizing depths.

"I'm sure Cooper is missing you tonight."

Aiden chuckled. "Probably not too much. He has Harley keeping him company. Zach is dog-sitting at my place while I'm out."

Mr. De Luca returned and took their order for the

main course. Lindsay ordered the lasagna and Aiden the calzone.

"It's nice to be able to order my own meal," Lindsay said with a chuckle.

Aiden's eyebrows furrowed together. "Who would order for another person?"

With a heavy sigh, Lindsay replied, "You'd be surprised. Erica signed me up on one of those dating sites, and the first 'match' I went on a date with did just that."

"No way," Aiden said in disbelief. "Seriously?"

"As sure as I'm sitting right here, and his follow-up for when I tried to place my order was to tell me I didn't need to diet."

"Wow, there are definitely some weirdos out there. I can't believe he had the nerve to say that to you."

Lindsay shook her head. "It's probably one of the reasons I reacted so harshly to our first date. I was tired of going out on bad ones."

"Again, I'm so sorry for that." Squeezing her hand, he stated tentatively, "I hope I'm making up for it tonight."

"You certainly are," Lindsay said with an alluring smile.

In that moment, Aiden knew he wanted to keep that smile on her face no matter what it took.

"I've been meaning to ask you, how is Alex doing?"

Lindsay pinched her lips together as tears formed in the corner of her eyes. "Not great. He won't tell anyone what happened, but he got a black eye at the shelter group home. I'm doing everything I can to get him out of there, but it's been frustrating. At least I just found out there's a potential new family being approved to foster, and I have Alex lined up to be their first kid."

"I hope it works out," Aiden stated. "He's a good kid and deserves to be in a happy home. Tell him 'hi' from me the next time you see him."

Their food arrived a few minutes later. After a couple of bites, Aiden asked, "You mentioned earlier that you love this place. Any particular reason?"

Although a smile remained on Lindsay's face, a sadness crept into her eyes. "My parents used to bring me here for my birthdays." Glancing away, she added, "At least until my mom died. Then my father didn't feel much like celebrating anything and we stopped coming."

"I'm sorry to hear that. If I had known it would bring up painful memories, I wouldn't have brought you."

"It's not your fault, and I loved coming here."

The rest of the meal passed with easy conversation until they were both finished. Mr. De Luca appeared with a plate of decadent sweets. "Can I offer you dessert?"

Aiden looked across the table and said, "It's up to the lady."

Lindsay bit her lip in an endearing manner before responding. "I really shouldn't, but I'm a sucker for tiramisu."

"You heard the lady; one piece of tiramisu, please," Aiden stated.

With a nod, Mr. De Luca said, "Coming right up."

"Aren't you going to have dessert?" Lindsay asked.

"I'm not much of a sweets person. Now, you put a pizza in front of me, and it's a different story."

Lindsay laughed, causing her nose to crinkle and her eyes to sparkle. The lilt of her laughter made Aiden's heart fill with joy. He liked making her happy.

The tiramisu arrived, and Lindsay gingerly took a bite. Looking up, she asked, "You're sure you don't want a bite? It's delicious."

"There's only one fork," Aiden noted.

With a shrug, Lindsay said, "That's okay. I'm not a germaphobe. We can share."

If she were offering to feed him, who was he to object? "Sure, since your offering."

Lindsay pushed her fork through the dessert and then reached out towards Aiden. He moved forward and took the bite. Their eyes locked over the candlelit flowers before his eyes dropped to her mouth for a moment and then flickered back up to her eyes. Aiden felt a quickening in his chest as his palms started to sweat. It was all he could do to keep from leaning across the table and claiming her mouth with a kiss.

Lindsay's cheeks turned pink from the intimate moment and her eyes dropped to the table. She finished the rest of the dessert without either of them commenting on the exchange, yet the tension was palpable.

Mr. De Luca arrived with a brown bag in his hand. "Here's a little something for Cooper," he said as he handed Aiden the to-go food before they exited the restaurant.

Aiden took Lindsay home and walked her up to her door. "I had a great time tonight. When can I see you again?"

She tilted her head up, letting her eyes meet his. Her long eyelashes fluttered up and down, like butterfly wings. "I'm going to be at church tomorrow. Are you planning on coming?"

"That's not exactly what I had in mind," Aiden

said with a chuckle, "but yes, I plan on coming to church tomorrow."

Her mouth turned up in a playful smile as she said, "Good. We can discuss our next date then."

His mouth started to descend to hers as the intoxicating scent of vanilla swirled around him. But before their lips could touch, Aiden's cell phone rang. He looked down and saw it was dispatch.

"I have to go," Aiden said with disappointment. "I'm on call and work needs me."

"That's alright. I'll see you tomorrow morning."

Aiden turned and walked away from Lindsay, knowing thoughts of her were going to fight to distract him all night.

TWENTY-ONE

Standing on the steps to Clear Mountain Assembly, Lindsay had to force herself not to fidget as she watched Aiden walk up the path. He looked handsome in his grey pants and black shirt.

Apparently, she wasn't the only one who noticed. Several women plastered on flirtatious smiles as they tried to make eye contact with him, but his eyes remained resolutely focused on Lindsay.

His lack of reaction to the other women made Lindsay feel special. She was aware that with his smoldering good looks and attractive job, he could date most any girl he wanted. It was flattering to know she was the center of his attention.

"Good morning, Aiden."

"Good morning, Lindsay."

"How did work go last night?" Lindsay asked.

"It was a missing hiker, but by the time I got there, the wife called the substation and told us her husband got home. Apparently, he dropped his phone down a ravine and couldn't make a call."

"Well, I'm glad to hear it turned out okay," Lindsay stated.

"Me too."

"I was thinking—even though this isn't your first time here—you probably didn't get much of a chance to see the place last week. You want me to give you a tour?"

Aiden nodded. "That would be great."

Lindsay guided Aiden through the front doors of the church and into the foyer. At the front desk stood Stacy, who greeted both of them with a welcoming smile. "Good morning, Lindsay. I see you have a guest." Then after a moment longer, her eyebrows raised up in recognition. "Wait, didn't I see you here last week?"

"You did, indeed," Aiden answered with a grin. "My name's Aiden O'Connell."

She clasped her hands together in excitement. "Aren't you the police officer who has been mentioned in the newspaper several times?"

With a nod, Aiden confirmed, "Yes, that's me."

"I can't wait to tell Pastor Steve we have a true local hero in our midst. You have to meet him after service."

"Stacy, that's sweet of you to offer, but we don't want to make Aiden uncomfortable."

"It's alright. If the pastor has the time, I would enjoy meeting him."

Lindsay's head snapped to the side, her eyes watching Aiden's face to make sure she hadn't mistaken what she'd heard. Sure enough, he seemed to be genuinely happy.

"I'm going to show him the rest of the church before service starts, Stacy."

The woman nodded and let them go. Next, Lindsay took him down the children's wing of the church which was on the left side of the building.

"This is the nursery," she pointed to the first room, "which is where I work on Sundays." She continued down the hall. "This is the toddler room," she gestured to the second door. She finished showing him the children's church and the junior and senior high meeting rooms.

After reaching the end, they made their way back up the hall and entered the lobby again.

"What's on the other side of the building?" Aiden inquired.

"The church offices."

Aiden nodded. "Makes sense."

Lindsay glanced down at her watch and noticed it was five until nine. "Service is going to start soon. Erica said she would save us seats, so we should go find her."

TWENTY-TWO

The worship music poured out of the speakers just as Aiden and Lindsay found their spots next to Erica a few rows from the front of the sanctuary. Erica smiled at them before turning her attention back to the stage.

Aiden never was one for public singing, but the music was enticing. He found himself singing along as he read the lyrics on the giant screens on either side of where the musicians played.

When the music ended, Pastor Steve took to the stage. "Hello, Clear Mountain Assembly. It's good to see all of your smiling faces looking back at me this morning. We're continuing our series entitled, 'God's Handiwork.' Most of you know, I have two daughters, my oldest, Christine and my youngest, Marybeth. Like most siblings, they're extremely competitive. Marybeth is always trying to keep up with Christine. In most cases, Christine is usually better at everything simply because she is older, that is until recently when my Marybeth tried out for the soccer team. She's good. I mean really good, and far better than Christine ever was at the sport. This of course made Christine seethe with jealousy. She wondered why God didn't make her good at soccer too. She began being mean to Marybeth, refusing to go to her games and picking at her constantly. I ended up having to sit them down and explain that God makes all of us different, but that doesn't mean any one person is better or more special than another. We all just have different gifts and God gave each of us our gifts so we will use them for His kingdom.

"Think about it, the same God who created the stars in the sky, the oceans and millions of galaxies looked at the entire universe. He also decided there needed to be a Christine, a Marybeth, and a you, to make His design complete. How magnificent does that make each of us?"

The powerful words penetrated Aiden's heart and he realized that God made him the way he was so that he would want to help people. It made him profoundly proud that God would put that much trust in him.

As the service concluded, Aiden felt a peace in his heart. He realized he had missed going to church.

"What did you think of the message?" Lindsay asked Aiden.

"The pastor's words made me think about why God created me. It gave me a new perspective. I'm glad I came today."

"Me too."

"Do you want to go out to brunch?" Aiden asked, not wanting his time with Lindsay to end.

"I'd like that, but I work in the nursery during second service."

Aiden felt his heart clench in disappointment. She gave him a sympathetic smile, then added, "But I promised you we'd discuss our next date. How about you take me out this coming Friday?"

"I'd like that. Do you mind if I text you throughout the week?"

"Of course not. I think that would be nice."

Aiden watched as Lindsay headed towards the children's wing. He couldn't wait to send her his first text.

TWENTY-THREE

"Is this the place?" Alex asked as Lindsay watched him in the rear-view mirror as he placed his face against the window in excitement.

"It sure is," Lindsay said in an upbeat tone. "The Winters don't have any children of their own, so you're going to have the run of the place."

"I've never been in a home without other kids in it," Alex said with apprehension. "It's gonna be weird to have them focusing only on me."

"Yes, but that's a good thing," Lindsay stated with conviction. "You should try to take advantage of this time with them as it probably won't last forever. They stated on their application they're willing to take multiple children."

As Lindsay parked her car, she said, "I've been meaning to tell you that Officer O'Connell told me to tell you 'hi.'"

His eyes grew wide as a giant smile formed. "That's awesome." Then as if an idea popped into his head, he asked, "Are you two boyfriend and girlfriend now?"

"Whatever gave you that idea?" Lindsay asked, flustered.

"Why else would you see him again? Besides, he likes you and you like him too. It was so obvious at the carnival."

Lindsay could feel her cheeks warm under the observation. Leave it to Alex to point out something she was still in denial of. She was falling hard for Officer Aiden O'Connell, and it didn't seem to be one-sided.

Lindsay got out of the car, made her way around to the other side, and opened the back door. Alex hopped out, pulling his blue suitcase behind him.

"I hope they like me," Alex said, the concern audible in his voice.

"What's not to like? You're a great kid. Anyone would be lucky to have you."

"I wish you could just adopt me."

She didn't want to tell Alex how many times she had wished the same thing. She knew without a husband, she couldn't take on such a responsibility by herself. "You know if I could, I would."

"I know. It's just wishful thinking."

"Nothing wrong with wishing for something, Alex, because sometimes wishes do come true. You wished to get out of that shelter group home, and look, now you have a brand-new foster home with parents ready to take you in."

The pair made their way up the steps of the small cottage-style house. Lindsay knocked on the door, which immediately swung open to reveal a thin woman with brown hair and glasses.

"Hi," the woman said with a sugary sweet voice. "I'm Ashley, and this is my husband, Bob." Bending down, she added, "And you must be Alex."

Nodding, Alex reached out and wrapped his arm around Lindsay's waist.

"Alex tends to be shy in new environments," Lindsay explained.

"That's alright. We'll have plenty of time to get to know each other soon enough. Why don't you both come in?" Ashley offered. "We have cookies and lemonade on the kitchen table."

Alex's eyes darted up to meet Lindsay's. She nodded, "Go ahead, Alex. I'm right behind you."

As everyone made their way into the kitchen, Lindsay watched Bob. It was odd he was being so quiet. He didn't seem overly pleased to have Alex in their home. Had Ashley pressured him into this situation? It wouldn't be the first time that one foster parent was pushed by the other to foster when they either weren't ready or secretly weren't interested.

Ashley placed a cookie on a plate in front of Alex, then poured him a glass of lemonade. "Do you need to see Alex's room?" Ashley asked.

Something was bothering her about these two and Lindsay was glad she was required to check Alex's room. "Yes, that would be best."

Ashley headed down the small hallway, past two doors until she came to a final one in the back. She pushed it open to reveal a room painted light blue. It had a twin bed, a dresser, and nightstand. There was a toy chest at the foot of the bed along with a desk in one of the corners.

"Everything seems to be in order," Lindsay acknowledged. Turning to face Ashley, Lindsay pulled a list from her clipboard and handed it to her. "These are Alex's likes and dislikes, along with the list of the medications he has to take to stimulate his growth. I know the office probably already gave you a list, but I've known Alex a long time, and my list is more detailed."

Ashley took the list and slipped it into her pocket

without looking at it. "Thank you," she said as she pulled the door shut. "Is there anything else?"

Lindsay shook her head. "My direct cell number is also on the list, so if you have any questions or problems, just let me know."

Nodding, Ashley escorted Lindsay to the front door. "We appreciate you bringing him here."

"Of course. Can I say goodbye?"

Ashley glanced back towards the kitchen. "I think you should give my husband time to bond with Alex. Maybe it's best if you don't interrupt that."

Lindsay wanted to object, but she didn't have a legitimate reason to do so. It was important for Alex to start connecting with his new foster parents.

Turning around, Lindsay left Alex's new home and silently sent up a prayer that he would find happiness there.

TWENTY-FOUR

Aiden woke up thinking about Lindsay, just like he had every morning over the past week. He reached for his phone on his nightstand. Blinking on the screen was a final text from the woman who had taken up permanent residence in his head and, if he was willing to admit it, his heart.

Goodnight, Aiden. :)
Can't wait to see you on Friday night.

They had been texting back and forth throughout each day since the previous Sunday at church. His fingers hovered over the buttons to text her back. His ego told him to play it cool, but his heart won out.

Before he could rethink his decision, his fingers typed back.

Hey, Lindsay.
How's your day going?

A few moments ticked by before his phone lit up with a new text.

Good. Busy.
Have two new kids added to my case load.
Both sad situations.
My heart aches for them.

Aiden texted back:

I'm sorry to hear that.
I'll pray for strength for you
And a good home for the kids.

Where did that come from? It wasn't like Aiden to offer prayer, but it also wasn't like him to be going to church. Correction: it wasn't like him in the last few years, but before his parents died, he had been a devoted Christian.

Even though he had gone back to church to win over Lindsay, the moment he stepped into church he felt like a piece of his heart (the most important piece) was put back into place.

Since that moment, he felt an overwhelming desire to grow close to God again. He downloaded a Bible app on his phone and started reading every morning. He found himself turning on the Christian radio in the car and praying throughout the day.

Thanks, Aiden.
Got to go.
Have another appointment.

Aiden put down his phone and jumped out of bed to go take a shower. Even though L.T. gave him the day off due to all his overtime from call-outs, Aiden needed to go hit the gym and take Cooper out for a run.

Just as he was finishing tying his shoes, his cell phone rang. As he looked at the screen, he hoped it was Lindsay, but instead Dispatch's number blinked back at him.

He answered, "Hello, this is O'Connell."

"We have a missing female, Aiden," Deanna's voice said over the phone. "We need you to load up with Cooper and head over to the last known location."

"Will do."

Looking over at Cooper, who was laying on the edge of the bed, Aiden stated, "Guess we aren't making it to the park today, boy. Sorry about that."

With quick precision, Aiden removed his gym clothes and switched into his uniform. He grabbed his gear and placed Cooper on his leash before leaving his apartment.

~

WHEN AIDEN ARRIVED AT THE LOCATION, THE REST OF the search and rescue team was already present. Sergeant Burton was finishing giving out tasks to the other officers in the unit as Aiden approached.

"Glad you could join us, O'Connell," Sergeant Burton said sarcastically.

"Sorry, Sarge. It was my day off. I had to change out of my civilian clothes before heading over."

"Fine. You will be taking the south side of the grid near the school. Everyone else is already out searching. Here are the facts. The mother reported the sixteen-year-old female missing this morning, claiming the teenager had a tendency to spend the night at friends when the mother was working. The missing female routinely called to check in. When she didn't call this morning, the mother phoned around with no success of locating her. That's when the mother called us. The missing female's phone is not on, so we can't locate her via GPS. We checked with the school which verified she was in class all day yesterday, placing her abduction most likely in the afternoon. Through knock and talks, we verified her last known whereabouts. The missing female was last seen walking home from school yesterday afternoon. A neighbor witnessed the missing female being pulled into a section of the nearby forest by an assailant but didn't report the incident until knock and talks."

Sergeant Burton handed a purple t-shirt to Aiden. "Here is a piece of her clothing we got from the mother." Aiden took the shirt and continued listening as Sergeant Burton finished up. "You know that time is of the essence, so make each moment count."

Aiden reached out and let Cooper imprint on the shirt. After he was sure Cooper had the scent ready to track, he gave the command for Cooper to start their search. The pair made their way into the south side of the forest that backed the edge of the high school.

Cooper started his pattern of sniffing areas and then moving along until he found another area he wanted to inspect. Aiden kept his eyes peeled for any movement or clues.

About thirty minutes into their search, Cooper started barking furiously near a bush. Aiden rushed up and inspected the area. On the edge of the bush was a piece of clothing. Aiden pointed his flashlight, revealing a piece of pink and white cloth.

"Command, this is K-9 2, can you give me a description of what the girl was wearing at the time of abduction?" Aiden asked over the radio.

"K-9 2, the girl was wearing a pink and white striped top and blue jeans."

"Command, I have visual confirmation of a piece of the missing female's outfit. I'm at four clicks south of starting point. I'm marking location with an orange flag, and then continuing search."

"Copy that, K-9 2. We will send out forensics to that location to gather evidence."

Aiden bent down and rubbed Cooper's ears. "Good job, boy, but we still need to keep going. We need to find this girl."

Cooper took off running and started his pattern again. About fifteen minutes later, Cooper stopped near a cluster of boulders and started barking furiously.

As Aiden approached the spot, his breath caught in his throat. The instant he saw the girl's motionless body, Aiden knew they had found her too late.

He bent down next to her and didn't even need to

feel for a pulse. Her skin was ashy blue, and her eyes were fixed and hollow.

~

As Aiden left the edge of the forest and headed back over to the search's central command, Natalie Watts came barreling towards him, with recording device in hand. "Officer O'Connell, what do you have to say about the tragic outcome of this missing girl? According to my records, this is your first negative outcome since being with Clear Mountain Search and Rescue. Do you care to comment?"

Aiden gave Natalie a steely look before spitting out, "No, I have nothing to say on the matter."

"You don't feel at all responsible? You have nothing to say to the girl's family?"

Aiden pushed past Natalie and made his way into the taped-off perimeter. He headed over to his SUV and sat on the back edge of the open hatch. Cooper jumped up next to him and put his head in Aiden's lap. Absent-mindedly Aiden rubbed the dog's ears.

He couldn't shake the empty stare of the dead girl's eyes. No matter what he did, her haunting image came floating back to take over his mind.

Zach came over and sat down next to Aiden. "How are you handling all of this?"

"Not great. Did you hear Natalie Watts? She asked me how it felt to finally have a loss on my record? As if it wasn't bad enough what happened to that girl, but to have that reporter trivialize it in such a way, it makes my stomach churn."

"You got to let it go, man. Why don't you come out drinking with me? There's nothing a few beers can't fix."

Aiden shook his head. "I just want to go home. Maybe call Lindsay."

"Man, ever since you started seeing that girl, something has changed in you. You're not even seeing things clearly anymore. We both know that girl was dead the moment she was taken."

Aiden's head snapped up and his eyes glared at Zach. "No, I didn't know that. I honestly thought Cooper and I would find her alive."

"Well, I've been doing this a couple more years than you, which is probably why I don't let myself get invested in the outcome. It's easier that way."

"Easier for you, you mean. I don't want to end up jaded like you, Zach. I don't want to stop caring."

Surprisingly, Zach didn't seem offended. Instead, he shrugged and said, "Suit yourself. If you want to wallow in this, go ahead. If you change your mind, I'll be at The Lucky Penny."

TWENTY-FIVE

Lindsay looked at the blinking screen of her phone and read the text that just came in from Aiden.

I could use some prayer.
I found a missing girl today, but it was too late.

The words made Lindsay's stomach knot in empathy. It was hard enough dealing with children being displaced, she couldn't even imagine if one of them died while she was responsible for them.

Rather than text him back, Lindsay called instead. After the second ring, Aiden picked up. "Hey Aiden, how are you doing?" When he didn't answer right away, she added, "I know, dumb question."

"It's just . . ." She could hear the pain in his voice. "I couldn't save my parents, and this just brings up all those feelings of uselessness. I wanted to be able to save that girl."

"That's so tough, Aiden. I can't even imagine." Wanting to comfort him in person, Lindsay stated, "I'm coming over so we can pray."

"Thanks. I could use that."

Fifteen minutes later, Lindsay arrived on Aiden's doorstep. She rapped the knocker and a few seconds later, Aiden opened it.

Her heart lurched as she took in his disheveled appearance. His eyes were bloodshot and haunted.

"Come in," he offered, as he leaned against the edge of the door.

Lindsay slid past him and stopped just inside the entryway. Cooper came up and started licking her hand. Instinctively, she turned her hand over and began petting him.

Aiden turned to face Lindsay. "I just keep seeing her lifeless face staring at me. I can't get the image out of my head."

Reaching out, Lindsay gathered Aiden into her arms. "Dear Lord, right now, we just come to you and ask for your healing hand to fall upon Aiden's heart and mind. You made him to be caring and empathic, which are two of the attributes that make him so good at his job. You also help carry our burdens, so I ask that you take the weight of this day, of this loss, from Aiden. Give him a peace, a peace that surpasses understanding. Be with the family of the girl and comfort them during this most difficult time. We ask all of this in your precious name, Lord Jesus, Amen."

Aiden pulled back and gave a lopsided grin to Lindsay. "Thanks. I needed that."

"Do you want to go sit down for a while? I don't have an early morning tomorrow so I can stay for a bit."

Aiden nodded, taking Lindsay's hand and pulling her over to the couch. "I think I need to laugh. You want to watch The Three Stooges?"

Lindsay laughed as she shook her head. "I didn't see that coming."

"See what?" Aiden asked, confused.

"You being into classic slapstick comedy."

Aiden winked at her and said, "I think you'll find I'm just going to keep on surprising you."

As he sat down in the center of the couch and gathered her into his arms, he whispered in her ear, "This feels right."

TWENTY-SIX

A surprising side-effect happened the other night when Lindsay came over to his house and comforted him; a deepening of his emotional and spiritual connection with her.

Aiden texted her that same night and told her he wanted to start praying with her every morning before work and every evening before bed.

As he got ready to go pick her up for their surprise date, he said a prayer of gratitude to God for sending him Lindsay. He knew he had been unhappy with his life—he thought it was simply because he had been dating the wrong type of women—but now he knew it was because he had been closed off to God. Lindsay helped him see that, and he got the perfect woman in the bargain.

Cooper barked as he came into the living room. "That's right, boy. We're going to go see Lindsay. I bet you're as excited as I am to see her today."

He hooked the leash onto Cooper's collar and guided him out of the apartment and into his waiting mustang.

~

Lindsay finished tucking in her navy-blue t-shirt into her favorite pair of black jeans, then pulled on a pair of flats.

Aiden had texted her and told her to dress casual for their afternoon date. When she texted him back and asked what they were doing, he told her it was a surprise.

Flashes of their first date came to mind, but she reminded herself Aiden wasn't the same guy who took her to The Lucky Penny that first night. In a couple of weeks, she had seen a huge change in Aiden.

The doorbell rang, and Lindsay heard the door open, then Erica say, "Come on in. Lindsay will be right down."

Lindsay put on a dab of vanilla perfume behind both ears and then on her wrists, before grabbing her purse and coat off her bed.

As Lindsay came down the stairs, Aiden's smiling face greeted her. He looked good in a pair of blue jeans with an untucked black t-shirt under his black leather jacket. It was funny, the first date they went on, he wore almost exactly the same outfit, but for some reason, it didn't bother her this time.

"You ready?" Aiden asked with a grin.

"I guess as much as I can be since you won't tell me where we are going."

"You're going to love it. Hope it's ok, but I brought Cooper along for the outing too."

Giving him a skeptical look before putting on her coat, Lindsay thought about what his hint could mean. As they walked to the car, Lindsay contemplated the intriguing clue.

Cooper was sitting in the back seat of the Mustang with the front window cracked. As they made their way out, he put his paws to the window as his tail wagged in excitement.

A moment after Lindsay sat in the front passenger seat, she felt warm breath on her neck and the heavy sound of breathing. "Hey there, Cooper," Lindsay laughed, "It's good to see you too."

Aiden put his hand on Cooper's neck and gently pushed him backwards. "That's enough, boy. Give Lindsay some room." Turning to Lindsay, he apologized. "Sorry about that. He's used to doing whatever he wants when we're off-duty. He's spoiled that way."

"It's okay. I'm rather partial to dogs. We used to have several on the ranch."

"Do you miss it? Living on the ranch?"

"I did a lot in the beginning. I think the part that took me the longest to get used to was the noise of living in a town. Not that Clear Mountain is a big city, but it's much louder than living in the country."

"I get that, but I had the opposite reaction. Moving from Boulder to Clear Mountain, I had to get used to the lack of noise and activity."

"Why did you move from Boulder?" Lindsay asked.

Aiden's eyes flickered over to her for a moment then back to the road. "I was engaged in Boulder and my ex-fiancée left me for a police captain. There was too much baggage for me there. I wanted to start over, so when a spot opened up on the Clear Mountain Search and Rescue, I jumped at the chance to transfer."

"I'm sorry to hear that, Aiden." With a smile, she added, "Between you and me, she was a fool to give you up. You're the best."

The outlying buildings of Clear Mountain disappeared, and fields interspersed with trees started to appear. Aiden pulled down a dirt road parking near a house with a barn next to it. What were they doing here?

Aiden got out of the car and came around to help Lindsay out. He had Cooper's leash in his hand as he folded the seat forward, then clipped it onto Cooper's collar before he jumped out to join them.

"What's going on?" Lindsay inquired.

"You'll see." He guided her over to the barn and inside an older grey-haired man was standing, holding the reins of two saddled horses behind him.

"Lindsay, this is John Stockton. He owns this place."

Cooper raced up to John and nuzzled up to him; the older man rubbed the dog's ear in a familiar gesture. They obviously knew each other; what was the connection?

"It's nice to meet you, Lindsay." John handed the reins to Aiden and said, "We'll keep Cooper while you're out. Sue has been missing him."

"Thanks, John."

"Ready to go for a ride?" Aiden said as he reached out his hand to her.

Taking his extended hand, Lindsay asked, "What's going on? How do you know him? Why did you just let him take Cooper like that?"

"Let's get up on the horses and I will explain everything."

"But I don't have a pair of boots and my flats won't work," Lindsay stated with apprehension.

Aiden snapped his fingers as a grin formed. "Hold on just a second. I forgot something back in my car." After handing her the reins to both horses, he took off for his vehicle. A couple of minutes later, he returned with a pair of boots in his hands.

"I asked Erica what size you wear," he said as he gave her the boots. "I wanted to make sure today was perfect. I know you haven't gotten to ride in a long time."

Tears formed in the corner of her eyes at the thoughtfulness. "Thank you, Aiden," she said as she took off her flats and slipped on the boots.

Both of them mounted up on the horses and headed out of the barn. They meandered along a trail on the outskirts of the south field.

"So, you told me you would explain how you know John Stockton."

"You don't let anything go, do you?"

"Most people like my tenacity," Lindsay defended.

"Oh, I'm not saying I don't. I find it endearing." Aiden grinned. "As for how I know John, his son, Brad Stockton, was Cooper's previous handler. Brad still lived at home with his parents on the ranch, so Cooper lived out here too."

Lindsay inhaled sharply. She thought the name Stockton had sounded familiar. Brad Stockton used to be one of the search and rescue members. He died when he fell off the side of a cliff when it gave way during a search. She remembered because the newspapers did a feature on him and the town had a huge memorial.

"I thought K-9s retired when their handlers died or retired?" Lindsay asked in confusion.

"Cooper was young. He had barely finished training when the accident happened and still had a lot of years left to work. The department did offer to retire him and let the Stocktons keep him, but John and Sue realized Cooper wouldn't be happy just living on the ranch. They knew their son would want the best for Cooper, so they declined. When I took the position as Cooper's new handler, I was told of the connection to the Stocktons, so I made the decision to bring Cooper out here at least twice a month so they can spend time with him. I know he's one of the last connections they have to their son."

Lindsay's heart swelled at the unbelievable generosity of Aiden. To think, when they went on their first date, she had mistaken his lack of planning as being inconsiderate. The truth was, he was a good man who cared deeply for others, he just wasn't very good at dating, until lately.

"Aiden O'Connell, you might be the most wonderful man I have ever known."

"Thank you, Lindsay Wright. Coming from you, that's a high compliment."

TWENTY-SEVEN

After they finished riding, they returned the horses to the barn and gathered up Cooper. Mrs. Stockton prepared a picnic for them, which Aiden graciously thanked her for before they headed out.

"Where are we going now?" Lindsay asked.

"There's a nearby creek I want to set our blanket by."

Cooper was off his leash and Aiden was carrying the blanket under his left arm with the picnic basket in the same hand. Reaching out, he took Lindsay's hand with his right one. Turning back around, he said as they started walking again, "I'm starving. I see the creek just up ahead."

Once they reached the bank, Aiden shook out the

blanket and placed it on the ground. They took positions on the blanket, and Lindsay helped take out the items from the basket.

They ate the sandwiches and nibbled on the cheese and crackers as they watched the swaying of the trees and listened to the birds chirping in the distance.

"Life is so peaceful out here. I think this would be the perfect place to raise a family. Do you ever think about having kids?" Aiden asked.

"All the time," Lindsay stated. "It's actually the reason my last boyfriend and I broke up."

Aiden turned to face her and placed his hand on top of hers. With irritation, he said, "Let me guess, he didn't want kids. I want you to know, that's not an issue for me. I want to have a family."

He could feel her body stiffen under his hand as worry filled her eyes. "I wish that were the case. It was just the opposite." She paused for a moment, and her eyes dropped to the ground. "I can't have kids. My doctor told me because of my medical condition, I won't ever be able to carry a baby past the second trimester."

Aiden placed his hand under her chin and lifted her eyes to meet his. "I said I want a family. I didn't say I cared how I got one. I would love to adopt children given the opportunity."

Lindsay leaned her head on his shoulder and sighed in contentment. "You have no idea how good it is to hear that. Ever since Rick broke up with me over it, I thought no man would ever want to be with me once they knew the truth."

"All I care about is a future with the woman I adore." Pulling back, he added, "For the record, that's you."

She laughed, causing her whole face to light up in the most adorable way. Taking her into his arms, Aiden leaned down and pressed his lips against hers. The warmth of her skin against his spread across his whole body.

Lindsay's lips tasted like cherry Chapstick with a hint of vanilla. Aiden deepened the kiss as Lindsay leaned into it, wrapping her arms around his neck.

He didn't want to stop but he knew if he didn't, they would end up crossing a line. He respected her too much to let that happen.

Reluctantly, Aiden shifted away from Lindsay. "It's getting dark. I think we should head back into town."

Nodding in agreement, Lindsay helped Aiden clean up the picnic before they returned to Clear Mountain.

TWENTY-EIGHT

After finishing a long meeting at the office, Lindsay sat at her shared desk with one of the other regional social workers. Lindsay was grateful she was finally able to tell her boss she found a permanent placement for Mandy. Her mother didn't want to make the adjustments necessary to get Mandy back. Rather she opted to give up her parental rights, deciding she would rather go motorcycle riding cross-country with her new boyfriend than be a mother. One would think the little girl's sweet disposition and young age would've made it easy to find her a home, but foster parents were in short supply.

Lindsay's exhausted mind begged for something to wake it up. The travel mug of coffee from her drive in from Clear Mountain beckoned, but it had been hours since she arrived in Boulder.

Though tempted to take a swig, she knew it must be stale. She could head over to the break room for a fresh cup, but that would require getting up and her body didn't want to comply.

Didn't she have an energy bar in her purse? Pulling it out from the bottom drawer of her desk, she pushed her hand into her purse and rummaged around. As her hand brushed her phone, the vibration caught her attention.

Pulling her phone free from her purse, she glanced down at the blinking screen. Three missed calls from an unknown number and a new voicemail. She clicked over to the voicemail screen; the message was from the same number. It must be important.

Lindsay clicked the play button and put the phone to her ear.

"Miss Lindsay, this is Alex . . . I want you to come get me . . . I don't want to be here. Mr. Winters started . . . it doesn't matter what he did, I just . . . I'm scared, and I don't know what will happen next time." There was a sudden sound in the background, like a slamming door. Alex continued, whispering in a rushed and fearful voice, "I gotta go. Just come as quick as you can."

Abruptly the voicemail ended. Lindsay's hand

dropped from her ear and the phone tumbled to the top of the desk. What was that all about? What was Mr. Winters doing that upset Alex so badly? He sounded so scared. If it was any other child, she might chalk the call up to being dramatic—it wouldn't be the first time something like that happened—but she *knew* Alex, and he wouldn't react that way unless it was bad.

She checked the time of the voicemail. It was over an hour ago. She quickly dialed the number, but there was no answer. It would take her thirty minutes to get back to Clear Mountain. Grabbing her purse and coat, Lindsay rushed from the office.

When Lindsay arrived at the Winters' house, she paused to pray before getting out of her car. "Dear Lord, direct my steps. Show me the truth of what is going on. Help me to help Alex. Amen."

Lindsay climbed out of the driver's seat and made her way to the front door. She rang the doorbell. A few seconds later, Ashley Winters opened the door. Her eyes widened with surprise, then fear, before she masked her reaction.

"How can I help you, Miss Wright?"

"I was hoping I could see Alex."

"You didn't call to let us know you were coming by."

Warning bells started to ring in Lindsay's head.

The woman was obviously displeased that Lindsay was there. Politely, she reminded her of the rules. "I'm required to do unannounced visits. I just want to check in on Alex. Can I see him?"

Mr. Winters came up behind Ashley, then pushed his intimidating frame between them, blocking her view. "You should probably come back later. The boy isn't here."

"Well, where is he?" Lindsay asked, controlling her voice and keeping her concern from showing.

Mr. Winters shrugged. "He asked if he could go to the movies with one of his friends from school. Ashley dropped him off there a few minutes ago."

Alex didn't have many friends at school, and even fewer that he would do something after school with. Somehow, Mr. Winter's explanation didn't make sense. Lindsay's eyes shifted to Ashley. From the woman's uncomfortable stance, Lindsay suspected they weren't telling the truth.

"Since I'm here, can I do a house check? It will keep me from having to come back and do it later this week."

Ashley looked up at her husband as if waiting for his cue. When he nodded, they both moved out of the way. Lindsay entered the house and started to look around. Nothing seemed out of place as she moved through the residence. She made her way to

Alex's room and went inside. The room appeared in order, but almost too perfect. Why weren't his toys played with? Or any dirty clothes in the hamper? Why was everything meticulous on the desk? The condition of the room looked as if someone had staged it for a photograph.

Lindsay noticed that on the shelf above his bed sat the box in which Alex kept his favorite toy soldiers. He had had the box since Lindsay first started managing Alex's case. He took it from each home. If Alex was going to hide anything for her to find, he knew she would know to look in the box.

She pulled the box down and opened it. Inside was a folded letter with her name on it. Not wanting to draw attention to the letter since she didn't trust Mr. Winters, Lindsay discretely stuffed the letter into her coat pocket.

After placing the box back in its place, she turned around to find the Winters standing at the entry to the room.

"Does everything meet your approval?" Ashley asked.

Lindsay nodded. "Thank you for your time. I'll come back soon to talk with Alex."

Once she was back in her car, Lindsay yanked the letter from her pocket and read the contents.

Hey

The dad yells alot. He gets angry when stuff mesy. I try my best be good. I cover my ears when he yells. Today he shook me. The mom told him to stop. He hit her. I went to hid in the woods.

Alex

Oh, no. This was all her fault. Her instincts had been right when she first met the Winters. Why didn't she listen to her gut? She knew why; because she didn't want to make any unfounded allegations against new foster parents and she was anxious to get Alex out of the shelter group home and into a permanent home where he wouldn't be bullied by the other boys. She had convinced herself that her instincts were wrong, and Alex had paid the price.

Lindsay looked out the car window. The sun was already setting. How long could a little boy survive in the Colorado forest with winter approaching? And he didn't know directions, so was he lost? Could he even find his way back if he wanted to?

Tears started to form in Lindsay's eyes, but quickly she blinked them away. She needed to focus on what to do.

Grabbing her phone, she called her boss. No

answer. She left a quick message detailing what happened and told her boss she was going to call the local police.

Her next call was instinctively to Aiden. He picked up on the second ring.

"Aiden, I need your help. It's Alex."

TWENTY-NINE

The fear that laced Lindsay's voice chilled Aiden to the bone. Something must be terribly wrong. "What's going on with Alex?"

"He tried to call me several times today, but I was in a meeting. He left me a disturbing voicemail making me worry he wasn't in a safe environment. I came to the residence for a well check, but he wasn't here. I asked to enter the home, and during my inspection, I found a letter from Alex detailing allegations of abuse. He's run away, Aiden; he took off into the nearby forest!"

Seething anger filled Aiden's veins. What was wrong with people? How could they hurt such a sweet and loving boy as Alex? He would make sure they were dealt with properly, but first he needed to focus on finding Alex.

"Text me the address. I'm going to call this in." He paused for a moment as concern for Lindsay's safety came to the forefront of his mind. "Don't approach the house again. Stay in your car and keep it locked. If they think you're aware of what happened, who knows what they're capable of."

"Okay. I'll wait for you in my car."

After hanging up the phone, Aiden jumped into his SUV, then radioed over the details of what was going on to dispatch.

"K-9 2, this is Search and Rescue 1. Be advised, the entire unit will be joining you in the search."

Aiden's heart filled with pride at the brotherhood he shared with his fellow officers. When one of their loved ones was in trouble, they all treated it like one of their own. Lindsay had become the most important person in his life, and his fellow officers knew it from the way he talked about her.

"Copy that, Search and Rescue 1. Thanks for the assist."

The familiar voice of Zach said over the radio, "You know we got your back, brother. See you in five."

Aiden arrived at the address and saw Lindsay's car parked outside. He jumped out of his SUV and made his way up to the driver's side window. Tapping on the glass, he must have startled Lindsay, because she jerked slightly as her eyes grew round. Then a pensive smile formed on her lips as she rolled down her window.

"What's our next step?" Lindsay asked.

"The rest of the search and rescue unit will be here momentarily. They want to help. In the meantime, I'm going to go and tell the foster parents I'm aware Alex ran away. I'm going to inform them I need a piece of clothing to start the search. Are there any other children in the residence?"

"No. They don't have any children of their own and Alex was their first foster child."

"Good. Hopefully they'll comply."

"What happens if they don't?" Lindsay asked, her voice riddled with worry.

"Let's hope it doesn't come to that."

Aiden walked to the front door of the house and knocked firmly. A few moments later, a burly man with a sour look on his face answered the door.

Looking Aiden up and down, the man asked in a gruff voice, "How can I help you, Officer?"

"I received a call that a foster child that resides at this residence has gone missing."

The man's eyes narrowed as his face turned red with anger. "I don't know what you're talking about.

I told that nosy, uppity woman that Alex is at the movies."

"Look, sir, I know for a fact that isn't the case. You can either stop lying now and help us find the boy, or this is just going to get worse for you."

"How dare you tell me what I should do!" The man started bellowing at Aiden. "You've got no authority over me."

The man started to move towards Aiden in a menacing manner. Aiden's hand reflexively moved towards his gun on his hip.

"Sir, you need to step back now," Aiden demanded as he moved backwards down the path.

Even as he gave the command, Aiden could tell the man wasn't going to listen. He continued forward, forcing Aiden to swiftly pull his gun from the holster and point it at the other man.

"Stop now, or I'm going to fire my weapon," Aiden yelled.

That must have gotten his attention, because the man stopped moving and raised his hands.

Aiden kept his gun leveled at the other man. "Sir, turn around and put your hands behind your back."

"Why? What did I do?" the man asked as he grudgingly did as he was ordered.

Aiden placed his gun back in its holster and took

out his handcuffs. "I'm detaining you for the course of this investigation."

As Aiden finished handcuffing the man, Zach showed up with Harley. "Do you need help?"

"No. I got him, but can I put him in the back of your car before I get Cooper?"

Zach nodded. "Do you want me to go in the house and get a couple of clothing items for the search?"

"Yes, go ahead and grab it. Alex is the only kid that lives in the residence."

Fifteen minutes later, Aiden had Cooper out of the SUV, and ready to search for Alex.

"Promise me you're going to find him, Aiden," Lindsay pleaded in a frantic tone as she placed her hand on Aiden's arm. "I don't know what I'm going to do if you don't."

"I give you my word, I'm going to do whatever it takes to locate Alex."

"What can I do?" Lindsay asked.

"Pray."

Nodding, Lindsay stepped back to let Aiden begin.

"You ready, boy? This one really matters. It's Alex." Giving the command to search, Aiden added, "Go find him, boy."

Cooper took off into the nearby forest and started his trained routine with Aiden following behind.

After about a half hour, Lindsay texted Aiden for an update.

How is it going?
Have you found any clues?

Aiden texted back.

Still searching.
Haven't found anything yet.

Lindsay replied.

But the sun is almost completely gone.
It's getting cold.
He can't be out in the cold tonight.

Even though Aiden was thinking the same thing—knowing that both the weather and animals of the forest would be a problem for the boy—he didn't want to make Lindsay's fears worse.

It'll be okay.
I'll find him.

Flashes of the dead girl from the previous week came crashing into Aiden's mind, causing doubt to flood his heart. He knew the only way to combat fear was faith. Silently, he sent up a prayer for God to help him.

Another fifteen minutes passed. Cooper started barking and circling around a large pine tree. Aiden sprinted to the location.

Curled up in a ball at the base of the tree was Alex. Aiden bent down and reached out, gently stirring the boy awake.

"Alex, it's Officer Aiden."

The little boy rubbed his eyes as he asked groggily, "Is Cooper with you?"

On cue, Cooper started to bark, then moved over and began licking the boy's face.

"Does that answer your question?"

Alex began to giggle but flinched a moment later. "My leg hurts."

Aiden bent down and examined the leg. There was no external damage, but the ankle was swollen. "I think you sprained your ankle, Alex. I'm going to wrap it to help with the swelling."

Aiden pulled a roll of gauze from his backpack and made quick work of bandaging the ankle.

"Let me tell everyone you are okay—Lindsay is beside herself worried about you—and then I'll get you out of here." Aiden pushed the button of his radio receiver and then spoke. "Dispatch, this is K-9 2. I've located Alex. He's good."

"Copy that, K-9 2, glad to hear it."

Aiden quickly pulled out his phone and sent a text to Lindsay.

I found Alex.
He's OK.
Will be bringing him out shortly.

"Alright, Alex. I don't think you should walk on that ankle, so I'm going to carry you out."

The little boy nodded as Aiden picked him up, cradling him in his arms.

Twenty minutes later, the pair, with Cooper beside them, emerged from the forest.

Lindsay rushed up to them with a huge smile, giving them both a hug. "I'm so glad you're okay, Alex." She glanced down at the boy's wrapped ankle and asked, "What's wrong with his foot?"

"It's nothing, Miss Lindsay. Officer Aiden said it's only a sprain."

Lindsay's eyes filled with tears. "Thank you, Aiden. You have no idea how much this means to me."

"To me too. I care about this guy here," Aiden said as he gently squeezed the boy in a hug.

"Can you put me down? It's not very manly to be carried around by another dude, you know," Alex stated.

Both Aiden and Lindsay started laughing. Alex looked confused. "What? What's so funny?"

Aiden walked over and put Alex into the front seat of his SUV. He turned to face Lindsay, but before he could say a word, a thin woman with brown hair and spectacles approached them. Though she looked to be only in her mid-thirties, her stern expression called to mind an elderly nanny.

"Lindsay, do you have the letter which Alex Sterling wrote you?" she asked with an authoritative voice.

Nodding, Lindsay pulled it out of her coat pocket and handed it to the woman, who promptly unfolded it and quickly read the contents.

The woman looked up at Aiden and asked, "Is this the officer who found Alex Sterling?"

Again, Lindsay nodded. "Joyce Falton, this is Officer Aiden O'Connell. Aiden, this is my boss. Joyce is the head of the Boulder County Child Protective Services."

"Thank you for doing your job, Officer O'Connell,"

Mrs. Falton stated with no emotion in the words. "We would have been in a whole heap of trouble if you hadn't. It's bad enough the media is going to have a field day with the story. Considering everything, it's in everyone's best interest if Bob Winters is arrested."

"He's already in custody in the back of my partner's car. We planned on making his arrest official after we found Alex."

"Good." Turning to Lindsay, she added, "Additionally, the Winters' license to foster is being revoked, pending the outcome of the investigation into the situation that led up to Alex Sterling running away. Lindsay, make sure Alex returns to the shelter group home tonight. In the meantime, I'm going to go oversee the arrest of Bob Winters." Joyce Falton turned around and headed towards Zach's SUV.

"She's a formidable woman," Aiden observed.

"Indeed, but she does genuinely care about the children in our care."

"I'm betting not as much as you," Aiden stated with admiration.

"I love all my kids so much. I was so worried while you were in that forest." Lindsay placed her hands on his chest and looked up into his eyes. "I don't know what I would have done if anything happened to either of you."

"But nothing did," Aiden assured, "because God was watching over us."

"I'm so glad God brought you into my life."

"Me too," Aiden said before he leaned down and seared her lips with an adoring kiss.

THIRTY

The last couple of weeks had flown by. Aiden and Lindsay spent their evenings together and their weekends involved in church activities. They also visited Alex together whenever possible.

This afternoon, Aiden was taking Lindsay horseback riding again. The snow had finally let up, then melted, giving a window of time to be outdoors. They decided to take advantage of it.

As Lindsay sprinted out the door and hopped into Aiden's Mustang, he gave her grin. "Did I mention you look really good in jeans and a t-shirt?"

Lindsay laughed. "Every time I wear them."

"Well, it's just as true as the first time I said it."

"I don't see Cooper today," Lindsay noted.

"He's spending time with Harley and Zach. With Harley being sick for the past week, Cooper's missed her."

"It's so sweet how much they like each other."

Aiden nodded. "Cooper moped all week while she wasn't working."

"At least she's back now. Plus, he gets today with her. Although, I'm sure the Stocktons will miss seeing Cooper."

"Yes, but they'll understand. They're good like that."

A short time later, they arrived at the Stockton ranch. Just like before, John Stockton was standing in the barn with two saddled horses. He smiled at them as they approached. "Hello, Lindsay, Aiden."

"Hi, Mr. Stockton," Lindsay greeted in return.

"Now what did I tell you about calling me by my first name."

Lindsay could feel her cheeks turn red from the correction. "Sorry about that, John. I promise I'll get it right next time."

John chuckled. "It's alright, Lindsay. I just want you to think of us like family, just like Aiden here does," John stated as he patted Aiden on the back with his free hand.

"Thank you, John," Lindsay said. "I'd like that too."

"Now, you go enjoy your ride, and take your time." John handed over the reins to them before exiting the barn.

The duo mounted up on the horses and took off for the nearby creek. Knowing it would be cold, they had prepared with thick jackets, hats and gloves. Despite the chilly weather, the day was perfect.

~

"LOOK AT HOW BEAUTIFUL THE MOUNTAINS ARE TODAY," Lindsay smiled. "The tops are still covered in snow."

"They are beautiful, but not as beautiful as you," Aiden said with admiration. Bringing his horse to a stop, he dismounted and helped Lindsay do the same. Aiden tied off the horses to one of the nearby trees, then turned to face her.

"Lindsay, every moment I spend with you, I realize it's never enough. I hate when we're apart."

"I feel the same way," Lindsay confirmed.

"I can't imagine not spending every moment of every day with you for the rest of my life."

Lindsay's heart started to flutter in anticipation as she realized Aiden was about to propose.

"I know we haven't officially been together long, but I also know it doesn't matter because you're the one for me, Lindsay Wright." Aiden got down on one knee and took Lindsay's hands in his own. "Will you do me the honor of being my wife. Will you marry me?"

"Yes! Yes, I will marry you, Aiden O'Connell," Lindsay shouted with joy.

Jumping up, he pulled her into his arms and kissed her. Pulling back, a confused look crossed his face.

"What is it?" Lindsay asked.

"In all the excitement, I forgot to give you this." Aiden reached in his pocket and pulled out a ring box. He opened it to reveal a square-cut diamond ring.

Lindsay inhaled sharply. "It's beautiful."

"Can I put it on?"

"Of course," Lindsay said as she gave him her left hand. He slipped the ring on.

"How did you get the size right?"

"Erica. She's good at helping me get your sizes right."

Lindsay laughed. "It seems I owe her a 'thank you' when I get home."

Pulling her back into his arms, he said, "I have one more thing I'd like to discuss with you, future Mrs. O'Connell."

"What's that, Mr. O'Connell?"

"I know we've talked about wanting to find a

family to adopt Alex. What if we were that family? What if we adopted him?"

"Do you really mean that?" Lindsay asked as tears formed in her eyes.

"I do. I want a big family, and I want that family to start with you and Alex. The thing is, I think we should speed up the wedding so Alex can move in with us as soon as possible. That way, we can foster him while the paperwork goes through."

Aiden tried to read Lindsay's face. He didn't think she was the type of woman who needed a big wedding. He also didn't want to deny her one if she did want it. When she didn't respond right away, he said, "If you're wanting a big wedding—"

"That's not it. I agree with everything you're suggesting. I just . . . I just can't believe how blessed I am that God brought you into my life, Aiden O'Connell." She leaned up and kissed him soundly on the mouth. "Let's do this. Let's get married as soon as possible, so we can go get our boy."

IT'S NOT QUITE THE END!

~

Did you enjoy — **Lawfully Adored**? You won't want to miss the rest of the books about K-9 in the series from — Lorana Hoopes, Ginny Sterling, Elle E. Kay, and Evangeline Kelly.

Turn the page for a sneak peek of the next K-9 stand alone book, *Lawfully Protected,* by Evangeline Kelly releasing May 8, 2018!

Still want more? Coming soon: Zach's story in the new spin-off series, Clear Mountain Romances, by Jenna Brandt.

Zach and Erica met at their best friends' wedding, but Zach's obnoxious behavior caused Erica to avoid him. Something about her caught Zach's attention, because he can't stop thinking about her. Yet, he knows he blew it and doesn't know how to fix it.

Six months pass without either of them finding a successful relationship. The opposites encounter each other again at their friends' baby shower. This time, Zach is on his best behavior, but Erica makes it clear, she won't date a non-Christian. Zach makes the choice to brave church to hopefully entice Erica to take a chance on him. He joins Aiden and his family at Clear Mountain Assembly where Erica goes to church as well.

Over the next few months, Aiden comments that Zach is changing into a better man. Gone is his bachelor lifestyle and endless parade of women. Erica must have noticed too, because she agreed to finally go out with him.

Want to find out what the future holds when two opposites attract? Then make sure to read the first book in the Clear Mountain Romances coming soon.

PREVIEW - NEXT BOOK IN SERIES

Evangeline Kelly's *Lawfully Protected*

If I ever got married, it would be to a man who loved cats.

Snowball, my white Himalayan kitty, stared at me with her beautiful blue eyes, and then rubbed herself against my leg, purring like she was on cloud nine. Cats, despite their bad reputation, were easy to please. You just had to know how to handle them. They weren't like dogs, letting anyone pet them—in some cases even a burglar. No, cats were more discriminating creatures, and they figured out very quickly if you were worth their attention. Once they decided you were good enough, they would follow you anywhere—literally.

"Don't you worry," I crooned. "Mama's going to buy you that outfit."

Stooping down to pet behind her ears, I stroked her soft fur and checked the time. I'd promised Jane from the local buy and sell Facebook group that I'd meet her husband in fifteen minutes at Rooster's Nuggets, a local fast food restaurant. I regularly bought used items from that group and even though they came second hand, most of the items were top quality.

Normally, when someone wanted to purchase something from the site, they would stop by the seller's home. Maybe it made me untrusting, but I didn't feel comfortable going to a stranger's house if I didn't have to. I'd read too many stories about serial killers finding unsuspecting victims that way, and I had a knack for attracting strange characters. It was better to be safe than sorry. Thankfully, Jane understood my uneasiness and had arranged to have her husband meet me at a neutral location.

Thank goodness it was Friday, and after a long day at work, I was looking forward to a little levity.

Seeing that outfit on Snowball would crack me up. She would look just adorable in that blue crocheted bodysuit and hat to match.

Clucking my tongue, I picked up one of Snow's toys and led her over to her bed so she wouldn't follow me outside when I left. She seemed content to play, so I headed to the front entrance and swung open the door. A man stood on the porch, hand held high as if about to knock, and he wore a shirt that said: Sadie's flower shop.

"Hello, can I help you?" I asked.

"Delivery for a Miss Allison McBride. Is that you?"

A wave of uncertainty washed over me as I surveyed the plant in his hands. It had lush green leaves and big red . . . lips. That was the only way I knew how to describe them—big puffy bloodshot smackers. Psychotria elata—that's what they were called. I'd just had a conversation about them the previous evening at dinner with my coworkers, Melissa and Walter, and Walter had even shown me a picture online. Maybe they were playing a joke on me. "Uh . . . yes, I'm Allison, but I didn't order—"

"Someone else ordered this for you, Miss McBride. It appears you have an admirer." He handed me the plant, and I took it, glancing down at the strange gift. It was beautiful for sure but not your typical flower bouquet from an admirer.

I was a career counselor at a private college, and Walter was one of the history professors there. Melissa worked in the administration office, and she'd known Walter for a while. Melissa and I regularly got together for dinner, and she had insisted Walter come along with us this time—said he had a little crush on me but not to worry because he was harmless.

He was at least twenty years older and not my type, so I'd been reluctant at first. Since she'd already invited him, I went along with it so I wouldn't hurt his feelings, though I'd instantly regretted that decision. He'd stared at me all evening with these huge bug eyes.

"This is from Walter Henley, right?" I asked, looking for a card.

The delivery guy smiled. "Sorry, Miss. The customer preferred to remain anonymous, and he didn't want to include a note. He said to tell you," he glanced down at a pad of paper in his hands, "you wanted to see this plant up close, and now I've made it possible for you." He snickered. "He paid quite a bit for this. We don't normally carry this plant—had to special order it."

Definitely Walter. After talking non-stop about the

Irish potato famine in 1845, he'd brought up the plant randomly in conversation—awkwardly referred to it as "Hot Lips." Apparently, they were actually referred to that way because no one went around saying, "I have a Psychotria elata plant."

Releasing May 8th

ABOUT THE AUTHOR

Jenna Brandt is a Christian historical romance author and she is branching into contemporary romance in 2018. Her historical books span from the Victorian to Western to WWI eras with elements of romance, suspense and faith. Her debut series, the Window to the Heart Saga, has become a bestseller and her new multi-author series, The Lawkeepers, is sure to be a fan-favorite. She is also an author in the First Street Church kindle world.

She has been an avid reader since she could hold a book and started writing stories almost as early. She has been published in several newspapers as well as edited for multiple papers. She graduated with her Bachelor of Arts in English from Bethany College and was the Editor-in-Chief of the newspaper while there. Her first blog was published on Yahoo Parenting and The Grief Toolbox as well as featured on the ABC News and Good Morning America websites.

Writing is her passion, but she also enjoys cooking, watching movies, reading, engaging in social media and spending time with her three young daughters and husband where they live in the Central Valley of California. She is also active in her local church where she volunteers on their first impressions team as well as writes for the church's creative team.

JOIN MY MAILING LIST

Join Jenna Brandt's Tribe and get a FREE story.

Join The Lawkeepers mailing list for alerts about the series.

ALSO BY JENNA BRANDT

The Window to the Heart Saga

Trilogy

The English Proposal (Book 1)

The French Encounter (Book 2)

The American Conquest (Book 3)

Spin-offs

The Oregon Pursuit (Book 1)

The White Wedding (Book 2)

The Christmas Bride (Book 3)

The Viscount's Wife (Book 4)

First Street Church Romance, WWI Trilogy

Love's Mending Embrace (Book 1)

Love's Unending Grace (Book 2, releasing March 2018)

Love's Perfect Place (Book 3, releasing summer 2018)

The Lawkeepers Series

Jenna Brandt's Lawfully Loved

Lorana Hoopes' Lawfully Matched

Elle E. Kay's Lawfully Held

Lorana Hoopes' Lawfully Justified

Jenna Brandt's Lawfully Adored

Ginny Sterling's Lawfully Yours

Under the Mistletoe (Christmas Anthology)

For more information about Jenna Brandt visit her on any of her websites.

www.JennaBrandt.com

www.facebook.com/JennaBrandtAuthor

www.twitter.com/JennaDBrandt

Signup for Jenna Brandt's Newsletter

ACKNOWLEDGMENTS

Since I can remember, writing is the only thing I love to do, and my deepest desire is to share my talent with others.

First and foremost, I am eternally grateful to Jesus, my lord and savior, who created me with this "writing bug" DNA.

In addition, many thanks go to:

My husband, Dustin, and three daughters, Katie, Julie, and Nikki, for loving me and supporting me during all my late-night writing marathons and coffee-infused mornings.

My mother, Connie, for being my first and most honest critic, now and always. As a little girl, sleeping under your desk during late-night deadlines for the local paper showed me what being a dedicated writer looked like.

My angels in heaven: my grandmother, who passed away in 2001; my infant son, Dylan, who was taken by SIDS four years ago; and my father, two years ago.

Lorana Hoopes for editing my book and being a wonderful critique partner.

To my Beta Bells for giving me insight and letting me know what to change and why. Your ideas helped make this a better book.

To my ARC Angels for taking the time to read my story and give valuable feedback.

To the Jenna Brandt Books Street Team, who have pounded the virtual streets on the internet, helping to spread the words about my books. Your dedication means a great deal.

To my partners in this adventure creating The Lawkeepers Series: Annie Boone, Kate Cambridge and Lorana Hoopes.

Made in the USA
Middletown, DE
08 September 2018